STOWAWAY TO MARS

From the vantage-point of the 1970s we are fortunate in being able to appreciate the magnitude of John Beynon's discerning vision. How right he was in anticipating, in *Stowaway to Mars*, that international rivalry would precipitate dramatic achievements in outer space. Admittedly, in the tradition of earlier tales of interplanetary endeavour, his British and American contestants were sponsored by private enterprise; only the Russian rocket was, in the natural order of things, a government undertaking. Furthermore, the stupendous costs involved have so far limited space exploration on a grand scale to the two Super Powers, and Beynon's main, and gloriously triumphant, competitor has been eliminated. This detracts nothing from the realism of a story which in other respects is remarkably close to the truth—or may well prove so before the century is out.

This now classic piece of science fiction first appeared in the British periodical *Passing Show* (which had earlier featured John Beynon's first novel, *The Secret People*), as long ago as 1936. It was presented as 'an epic serial of the last great exploration of all . . . by the man who writes half a century ahead of all the others'.

WALTER GILLINGS
August 1971

Also by the same author

The Secret People

and available in Paperback

Stowaway to Mars
(Formerly Planet Plane)

John Wyndham
writing as JOHN BEYNON

CORONET BOOKS
Hodder Paperbacks Ltd., London

Copyright © 1935 Executors of John Beynon
Harris
First published (as Planet Plane) by George
Newnes, Ltd., London
Coronet edition 1972
Second impression 1972

The characters in this book are entirely imaginary and
bear no relation to any living person.

This book is sold subject to the condition that it shall
not, by way of trade or otherwise, be lent, re-sold,
hired out or otherwise circulated without the publisher's
prior consent in any form of binding or cover other
than that in which this is published and without a similar
condition including this condition being imposed on the
subsequent purchaser.

Printed in Great Britain
for Coronet Books, Hodder Paperbacks Ltd.,
St. Paul's House, Warwick Lane, London, E.C.4,
by Richard Clay (The Chaucer Press), Ltd.,
Bungay, Suffolk.

ISBN 0 340 15835/2

CONTENTS

CHAPTER I

DEATH OF A STRANGER

JAKE REILLY, the night watchman, made his usual round without any apprehension of danger. He was even yawning as he left the laboratory wing and came into the main assembly hangar. For a moment he paused on the threshold, looking at the structure in the centre of the floor. He wondered vaguely how they were getting on with it. Mighty long job, building a thing like that. It hadn't looked any different for months, as far as he could see.

But Jake could not see far. The towering object of his inspection was so closely scaffolded that only here and there could the dim lights filter between the poles to be reflected back from a polished metal surface.

'Workin' inside it mostly, now, I s'pose,' he told himself.

He switched on his lamp and let its white beam wander about inquisitively. The floor plan of this, the central part of the building, was circular. Around the walls lathes, power drills and other light machine tools were disposed at intervals. The constructional work cut off his view of the opposite wall, and he moved round it, conscientiously conducting his search. He let his light play upwards, sweeping the narrow gallery which circled the wall, and noticing that the doors giving upon it were all shut. He sent the beam still higher, above the level of the dim, shaded lights, to the distant roof. There was a criss-crossing of heavy girders up there, supporting huge pulley blocks. The cables and chains depending from them came curving down, looped back out of the way now on to iron hooks on the walls. He tilted his lamp so that its bright circle ran down the curved metal side again.

'Like bein' inside a blessed gasholder, that's what it is,' he told himself, not for the first time. 'Pile o' money that thing must've cost, and I don't s'pose it'll ever go.'

A sudden sound caused him to stiffen. Somewhere there had been a faint clink of metal upon metal. He transferred his lamp to his left hand, and a large, black, businesslike pistol suddenly appeared in his right. He swung the light around, sweeping the dimmer parts of the place with its beam.

'Now then. 'Oo's there? Come out of it,' he ordered.

There was no answer. His voice boomed round the metal wall, slowly diminishing into silence.

'Better come out quick. I got a gun,' Jake told the dimness.

He began to back towards the door where the alarm button was situated. No good trying to get the man single-handed in here. Might chase him round and round that scaffolding for hours.

'Better come quiet, 'nless you want a bullet in you,' he said.

But still there was no reply. He was in reach of the alarm now. He hesitated. It *might* have been only a rat. Better be sure than sorry, though. He hung the lamp on the little finger of his pistol hand and reached, without turning, for the switch.

There was a sudden 'phut' somewhere in the shadows. Jake shuddered convulsively. The pistol and the lamp clattered together to the ground, and he slumped on top of them.

A dark figure slipped from behind the scaffolding and ran across the floor. It bent for a moment over the fallen watchman. Reassured, it dragged the body aside, and laid it inconspicuously behind one of the lathes. Returning, it kicked the lamp away, picked up the fallen pistol and slid it into its own pocket. For some seconds the dark figure stood silent and motionless, then, satisfied that there had been no alarm, it raised its arm and took steady aim at the nearest of the dim lamps. Four times came the muffled 'phut' as of a stick hitting a cushion, and each time it was followed by a not very different sound as an electric globe collapsed into fragments. In the utter darkness followed clicks which told of a new

8

magazine sliding into the pistol. Then, with a series of carefully shielded flashes, the intruder made his cautious way towards the central scaffolding.

A door of the balcony suddenly opened, letting a fan of light into the blackness.

'Hullo,' said a voice, 'what's happened to the lights? Where's that fool Reilly? Reilly! Where the devil are you?' it bawled.

The figure on the floor below delayed only an instant, then it raised its pistol against the man silhouetted in the doorway. Again came the muffled thud. The man above disappeared, and the door slammed shut. The man with the pistol muttered to himself as he continued on his way to the scaffolding.

He had barely reached it when a blaze of intense flood-lighting threw every detail of the place into view. He looked round wildly, dazzled by the sudden glare, but he was still alone. Again he raised his pistol, training it on one of the blinding floods. 'Phut!' There went one, now for the next——

But there was to be no next. The roar of an explosion, thunderous within the metal walls, made him miss his aim. He turned swiftly. There was a second roar. The impact of a heavy bullet spun him round and sent him crashing headlong against the foot of the scaffolding.

'Got him,' a voice announced.

The door in the gallery opened wide again.

'Damned lucky he didn't get you,' said another.

'Awkward angle for him. He hit the rail,' the first replied, calmly.

A babble of men's voices was heard approaching rapidly. A door on the opposite side of the ground floor was thrown back to reveal a tousle-headed, sleepy-eyed group. It was evident that the sound of shots had awakened them, and they had delayed just long enough to slip greatcoats over their pyjamas and to seize their weapons. One of the men in the gallery called down:

'It's all right. We got him. He's round this side.'

The two of them made their way along the gallery to the staircase while the newcomers crossed the floor. By the time they had descended there was a small crowd round the body of the intruder. The man who was kneeling beside it looked up.

'He's dead,' he said.

'How's that, Doctor? I didn't——'

'No, you got him in the shoulder, he knocked his head against one of the poles as he fell.'

'Damn. I'd have liked to have got something out of him. Anything to show who he is?' He looked round at the assembled men. 'Where the devil's that Reilly got to? Go and fetch him, someone.'

One of the group made off for the purpose. Close by the door he stopped at the sight of a foot protruding from behind the lathe mounting. He looked more closely, and called to the others.

'Here's Reilly. He got him, I'm afraid.'

The doctor rose from beside the first corpse and hurried across. One look at the watchman was enough.

'Poor old Jake, right in the heart.' He turned back to the tall man who had been on the gallery. 'What had we better do with them, Mr. Curtance?'

Dale Curtance frowned and hesitated a moment.

'Better bring them both up to my office,' he decided.

The doctor waited until the bearers had retired, closing the door behind them, then he looked across at Dale.

'What actually happened?' he asked.

Dale shrugged his shoulders.

'I know about as much as you do. I had been working late in here with Fuller. We didn't hear anything—at least, I didn't. Did you, Fuller?' The secretary shook his head. Dale went on: 'Then when we went out to the gallery the lights were out, and somebody using a silencer took a pot shot at me. Naturally, we went back and turned on the floods, then I potted him.'

'You don't know him?'

'Never seen him before—as far as I know. Have either of you?'

Both the others shook their heads. The doctor crossed to the body and continued the examination which had been cut short by the finding of the watchman.

'Not a thing on him,' he announced, after a while. 'Shouldn't be surprised if he turned out to be a foreigner; clothes aren't English, anyway.'

There was a considerable pause.

'You realize, of course,' the doctor added, 'that we shall have to have the police in?'

Dale frowned. 'We can't—er——?'

'No, we certainly cannot. Why, all the men in the place will know about it by now. It'd be bound to leak out pretty soon. And that wouldn't look too good. No, I'm afraid you'll have to go through with it.'

Dale was still frowning. 'Damnation! That means the end of our privacy. The papers will be splashing it all round. The place will be overrun with reporters sniffing into every corner and trying to bribe everybody. I wanted to keep it quiet for months yet—and now they'll get the whole thing. Oh, hell!'

Fuller, the secretary, put in:

'Does it really matter very much now? After all, we're well into construction—nobody else could possibly build a challenger in the time available. It doesn't seem to me that we've really much to lose—except our peace, of course.'

'That's true,' Dale nodded. 'It's too late for them to start building now, but we're going to be pestered and hindered at every turn. And once the secret's out, it won't all be unintentional hindering.'

The doctor paused in the act of lighting his pipe. He looked thoughtfully at Dale.

'It strikes me that the secret's already been blown. What do you suppose *he* was nosing around for?' He nodded in the direction of the black-suited corpse. 'He wasn't just a casual burglar, you can depend on that. Silenced gun, no marks of identification, knew his way about here. No, somebody's on to you already, my boy, and whoever it is sent a spy to get hold of some more details—or to do some damage.'

'But it's too late. Nobody could build in time. We shall have all our work cut out to finish by the end of September ourselves.'

'Unless,' said the doctor, gently, 'unless they are building already. Two can play at secrecy. One of the odd things about you men of action is that you so frequently forget that there are other men of action. Well, now I suppose we'd better call the police.'

CHAPTER II

DALE

DALE CURTANCE could not be called a man without fear. Not only because a man without fear is a man without imagination, but also because the old terrors die hard and the world has so multiplied the causes of fear that no one is left entirely unafraid. But, looking at Dale, at his six-foot, broad-shouldered form, his long arms with their strong, freckled hands, his blue eyes, cold and hard as ice, one could seem to see far back along a line of Norse descent to less complex ancestors: stern fighters who, sword in hand, feared nothing in this world and little in the next—for they honoured Odin only to secure for themselves an eternity of battle among the champions of Valhalla. Of Dale, their descendant into a world where the battle is not necessarily to the strong, nor even the race to the swift, it might truthfully be said that he feared less and dared more than his fellows.

But this is an age of hair-splitting. Many could be found to say that while Dale's Norse ancestors were physically courageous, they were spiritually cowardly— that the motive of their courage was the fear of losing a reputation for valour . . .

Dale should not have married—at least, he should not have married a woman of Mary's type. And inwardly Mary herself knew that now.

He should have swept up one of the worshipping little things he had thrilled in the past. He should have installed in his home one of those pretty little golden-heads whose hope it was, and whose perpetual joy it would be, that she was the chosen and the closest to the hero acclaimed by millions. The envy of those millions would have been her constant nourishment; she would have lived in the reflected blaze of his triumphs, and all might have been happy ever afterwards—or until Dale should break his neck.

Mary had not been a worshipper. She had not the temperament though she could not, at first, remain quite insensitive to the glamour of his success. It may have been her calm in contrast with the bubbling delight of the others which attracted him at their first meeting. He may have been in a mood which was tired of popular triumph and easy conquest. Whatever the cause, he fell very blindly in love with her. And Mary did not fall in love; she began to love him in a way which he never could and never did understand.

This morning, sitting up in bed with the newspaper spread across the untouched breakfast-tray, she went back over it all.

A swift wooing and a swift marriage. She had been swept by a word out of her calm life into an insane volution of publicity. Her engagement had been a time of pesterment by interviewers, offers for signed articles, requests from photographers, suggestions by advertisers. The Press had played the occasion up well: they had even taken her own wedding away from her and substituted a kind of public circus.

That she resented it, Dale never knew. He never seemed to feel as she did that the journalists' avidity for details was all but a violation of the decencies. And she had tried not to mind. It was inevitable that they should see things differently. The circle of her upbringing had been unostentatious folk who had neither suffered from nor wanted popular publicity. Dale, on the other hand, had been born practically on the front page of a newspaper—with a silver spoon in his mouth and a silver megaphone to announce his arrival. The first and, as it transpired, the only son of David Curtance, known far and wide, despite his personal antipathy to the phrase, as 'The Aerial Ford'.

Yes, Dale had been NEWS from the time of his birth.

They had splashed it about in large type: To David Curtance, the man who made the Gyrocurts—the Flivvers of the Air—the Multi-Millionaire, the world's paramount mass producer of aircraft, a son, Dale. No wonder publicity failed to worry him.

After their limelit honeymoon, the Press had let them go for a time. And though Mary could almost feel the journalistic eyes peering at her in the hope of scooping the first news of an impending 'happy event', more than two years had passed in comparative peace. Dale's name was to be seen only infrequently on the front pages. He had seemed to be well in the process of changing from a current to a legendary hero.

And now, this . . . !

Under the date, the tenth of March, 1981, ran the banner headline:

DOUBLE DEATH IN CURTANCE HANGAR

closely followed by:

TRAGEDY AT SPEED KING'S WORKS

Mary, frowning, read the fates of a night watchman and an intruder, identity at present unknown. The latter, it appeared, had been worsted by Dale himself in the course of prolonged and desperate duel. All readers would join with the Editor in his expression of thankfulness that the speed ace himself was untouched. She was wise enough now in the ways of journalism to discard a large percentage of the sensational wrapping. But the fact remained that two deaths had occurred, and Dale was once more on the front page. All her efforts at withdrawal had been nullified in a single night, and they were back again where they had been more than two years ago.

But, if the account made her irritable, it had been left to the final paragraph to arouse her real perturbation.

One of the effects of the tragedy has been to reveal that much secret experimenting has been lately taking place at the Curtance shops. We are informed from a reliable source that a new type of craft is already in an advanced state of construction though no details can yet be revealed. 'What is Curty going to do next?' is the question which many will ask themselves. Though Dale Curtance himself maintains strict silence on the subject, there can be no doubt that this new rocket 'plane is intended to contest yet another record. Whatever he intends to attempt with it, we know that not only our own good wishes but those of all our readers will go with him. 'Curty', who has done more than any other man to put England 'on top in the air', will find when he makes his come-back that no one has been allowed to usurp his place in England's Hall of Fame. Good Luck to you, Curty.

Mary pressed the bell-push beside her bed. To the maid who answered she said:

'Doris, tell Mr. Curtance I would like to see him at once, please.'

The girl hesitated.

'He's very busy, madam,' she said, uncertainly. 'The gentlemen from the newspapers——'

Mary raised herself on her elbows and looked out of the window. A number of gyrocurts and other small aircraft was dotted about the lawn and the field beyond. Odd that she had not noticed them arriving.

'Have they been here long?' she asked.

'Some of them nearly all night, I understand, madam, and the others came very early this morning. They've been waiting to see Mr. Curtance, and he only went downstairs a few minutes ago.'

'I see. Then perhaps you had better not disturb him at present.'

As the girl went out, Mary relaxed on her pillow, looking unseeingly at the ceiling. It was impossible, as she knew from experience, to tear Dale away from the pertinacious young men of the Press. The Public came first, and herself second. She reached out her hand for the newspaper and re-read the final paragraph. It had come! What a fool she had been to pretend to herself that it would not. She let the paper fall and lay thinking of Dale and herself.

When she had married Dale, she had partially understood him, and had managed to work up a sympathy with his interests. Now, she was forced to admit, she understood him better and had lost sympathy with those interests. In rare moments of complete frankness she admitted her jealousy of those other interests and her resentment of other people's share in him.

Ten years ago, when he was just twenty-four, he had won the first non-stop Equatorial Flight—and for that thousands of people had begun to idolize him. And it had only been the start of a fantastic record of success. He had gone on to triumph after triumph, collecting prizes and further acclamation in his spectacular career. Since then he had lowered the Equatorial record three times and still held it, together with the Greenwich to Greenwich Meridian record, and goodness knew how many more. Partly through luck, but mostly by hard work and endurance he had grown in the public view to the stature of a fabulous superman: the stuff of which the old world would have made a demi-god.

She had regretted, but accepted the fact that the mass could give him something which she as an individual could not. Curiously, it was his preoccupation with inanimate things which caused her more active resentment. Once, in a state of depression, she had confided to a friend:

'With Dale it is not people who are my rivals so much as things. Things, things, things! Why do men think so much of things? Big, restless and—to them—such absorbing things. Why are they always wanting to change and invent—more machines, more and more machines? I hate their machines! Sometimes I think they are the natural enemies of women. Often when I see a rocket-plane go by, I say to myself: "Mary, that is your rival—it can give him more than you can. It has more of his love than you have." ... No, it's not nonsense. If I were to die now, he would turn to his machines and forget all

16

about me in making them. But if his machines were taken away, he would not devote himself to me—he would mope and be miserable. I hate his machines. I'd like to smash them all into little bits. They frighten me, and sometimes I dream of them. Big wheels whirling round and round and long steel bars sliding up and down with Dale standing in among them, laughing at me because I can't get at him, and there are rows and rows of cogs waiting to grind me up if I try. All I can do is to stand there and cry while Dale laughs and the machines rattle at me. I hate them, I tell you. I hate them!'

It had not been wise, she realized now, to extract that promise from him—that he would give up racing rocket-planes and only enter contests for lightweights of the flipabout class. He had given it only grudgingly and it had fretted him though he had tried at first to hide it. Now she knew he was going to break it—so, apparently, did the newspapers.

Her thoughts were broken into by a crunching of gravel beneath hurrying feet. Voices, mostly male, shouted incomprehensible sentences to one another. There was a dull throbbing of engines followed by the whirr of revolving sails as the gyrocurts and other flip-abouts on the lawn began to take the air.

The door opened and Dale came in. He bent over and kissed her. Seating himself on the side of the bed, he took one of her hands in his own and apologized for his lateness. Mary lay back, watching his face. She heard scarcely a word that he said. He looked so young, so strong and full of energy; it made her feel that despite the ten years between them; she was the elder. Impossible to think of him as anything but an adventurous youth. It came to her with a sudden stab that he was looking happier than he had for a long time.

'Dale,' she interrupted, 'what did all those reporters want?'

He hesitated for a fraction of a second.

'We had a little trouble down at the shops last night. Nasty business. They wanted to know all about it, darling. You know how they're always after every little detail.'

She looked steadily into his eyes.

'Dale, please be honest with me. Weren't they much more interested in that?' She picked up the paper and pointed to the final paragraph. He read it, with a worried look on his face.

'Well, yes—perhaps they were.'

'And now that you've told the whole world, don't you think you might tell your own wife?'

'I'm sorry, dear. I wasn't telling anyone at all—nobody would have known anything about it for months yet if it hadn't been for that business last night. Then they were on to it at once—they couldn't be stopped.'

'Dale. You promised me you would give up rocket racing.'

He dropped his eyes and played with the fingers of the hand that he held.

'It's not exactly rocket racing——' he began.

She shook her head.

'But you promised me——'

He got up and crossed to the window, pushing both his hands deep in his trouser pockets.

'I must. I didn't know what I was saying when I promised that. I thought I could settle down and give it all up. I've tried, but I'm not cut out to be a designer of other men's machines. Hang it all, I'm still young. These last two years I've designed and built some of the best rocket-planes in the world—and then I've had to sit by like an old fogy of eighty while young fools lose races with them, crash them by damn bad flying and God knows what else. Do you think it's been easy for me to watch them being mishandled while all the time I *know* what they are capable of—and could make them do it? This last year has been just hell for me down at the shops; it's been like—like giving birth to one stillborn child after another.'

'Dale!'

'I'm sorry, Mary darling.' He turned back to her. 'I shouldn't have said that. But can't you see what it means to me? It's taking all my life away. Try to see it, dear. Look, all your life you've wanted the baby you're going to have; suppose you were suddenly told that you couldn't have it after all—could never have a baby at all. Wouldn't everything become worthless for you? Wouldn't the bottom just drop out of life? That's how I've felt. I promised you I would give up the thing I've wanted to do all my life—the thing I've been doing all my life until I met you. Well, I've tried, I've done my best, but I can't keep that promise . . .'

Mary lay silent. She did not understand: did not want to understand. He was selfish—and stupid. To compare a smashed machine with a stillborn child. Talking as if his passion for speed and more speed could be compared with the urge to bear a child. What nonsense! He spoke like a child himself. Why couldn't *he* understand what it meant to *her* . . . ?

He was going on now. Something about her creating with her body and he with his mind. That neither of them should be permitted to ban the other's right to creation. Well, she had never said that he should not create rocket-planes—only that he should not fly them. It was not fair . . . It was his child that she was going to bear. His child that was making her feel so old and ill . . .

'What are you going to do with this new rocket?' she asked at last.

'Have a shot at the Keuntz Prize,' he said, shortly.

Mary sat up suddenly. Her eyes widened in a horrified stare.

'Oh, Dale, no——' Her voice trailed away as she fell forward in a faint.

CHAPTER III

REPERCUSSIONS

TUESDAY'S evening papers made considerable play with Dale's announcement, but a citizenry hardened through the years to seeing the sensations of one day's end amended or ignored at the beginning of the next, received the news on Wednesday morning as a novelty. It was impossible to ignore the headlines which erupted from Fleet Street.

CURTANCE TO DARE DEATH FLIGHT

shrieked the *Daily Hail*.

'CURTY' TO ATTEMPT KEUNTZ PRIZE

roared the *Daily Excess,* and the *Views-Record* followed up with:

BRITISH AIRMAN TO CHALLENGE SPACE

The *Poster* and the *Telegram* printed leaders upon British pluck and daring with references to Nelson, General Gordon and Malcolm Campbell. (The *Poster* also revealed that Dale had once ridden to hounds.)

The *Daily Socialist*, after a front-page eulogy very similar to that in the *Hail,* wondered, in the course of a short article in a less exposed part of the paper, whether the cost of such a venture might not be more profitably devoted to the social services. The *Daily Artisan* told the story under the somewhat biased heading: 'Millionaire out for Another Million.'

The *Thunderer* referred in a brief paragraph to 'this interesting project'.

At nine o'clock in the morning the *Evening Banner* brought out special contents bills:

AIRMAN'S PLANS

To which the *Stellar* replied:

CAN HE DO IT?

At ten o'clock the editor's telephone in the *Daily Hail* offices buzzed again. A voice informed him that Mrs.

Dale Curtance wished to see him on urgent business.

'All right,' he said. 'Shoot her up.'

At ten-twenty he began to hold a long and complicated telephone conversation with Lord Dithernear, the proprietor of the Concentrated Press. At approximately ten-forty he shook hands with Mrs. Curtance and returned to his desk with a revised policy.

At eleven o'clock, Mr. Fuller, on behalf of Mr. Curtance, told an agency that he was in need of half a dozen competent secretaries.

At twelve o'clock one Bill Higgins, workman, employed upon the construction of the Charing Cross Bridge, knocked off for lunch. As he fed his body upon meat-pie and draughts of cold tea he regaled his mind with the world's news as rendered by the *Excess*. Working gradually through the paper, he arrived in time at the front page. There he was impressed by a large photograph of Dale Curtance skilfully taken from a low viewpoint to enhance the heroic effect. His eyes wandered up to the headline whereat he frowned and nudged his neighbour.

'What is this 'ere Keuntz Prize, Alf?' he demanded.

'Coo!' remarked Alf, spitting neatly into the Thames below. 'You never 'eard of the Keuntz Prize? Coo!'

'No, I 'aven't,' Bill told him. He was a patient man.

Alf explained, kindly. 'Well, this bloke, Keuntz, was an American. 'E 'ad the first fact'ry for rocket planes—in Chicago, it was, and 'e got to be a millionaire in next to no time. But it wasn't enough for 'im that 'is blasted rocket-planes was banging and roarin' all over the world; 'e didn't see why they couldn't get right away from the world.'

'Whadjer mean? The Moon?' Bill inquired.

'Yus, the Moon and other places. So in 1970 or thereabouts 'e goes and puts down five million dollars—what's more'n a million pahnds—for the first bloke wot gets to a planit—and back.'

'Coo! A million pahnds!' Bill was impressed. 'And

nobody ain't done it yet?'

'Naow—not likely,' Alf spoke with contempt. 'Nor never will, neither,' he added, spitting once more into the Thames.

At one o'clock two gentlemen with every appearance of being well fed were sitting down to more food at the Café Royal.

'I see,' remarked the taller, chattily, 'that that nephew of yours has more or less signed his death-warrant. Think he'll go through with it?'

'Dale? Oh, yes, he'll have a shot at it, all right. I'll say this for him, he's never yet scratched in any event if he had a machine capable of starting.'

'Well, well. I suppose that means you'll come in for a pretty penny?'

'Never count my chickens. Besides, Dale's no fool. He knows what he's doing. He might even make it, you know.'

'Oh, rot. You don't really believe that?'

'I'm not so sure. Someday someone's going to do it. Why not Dale?'

'Nonsense! Get to another planet and back! It's impossible. It is to this age what the philosopher's stone was to an earlier one. It's fantastic—chimerical.'

'So was flying—once.'

At two o'clock a young schoolmaster looked earnestly at his charges.

'This,' he said, 'is a history lesson. I wonder what history really means to you. I should like you to see it as I do—not as a dull procession of facts and dates, but as the story of Man's climb from the time when he was a dumb brute: a story that is still being told. If any of you saw the newspapers this morning, I wonder if it struck you as it struck me that within a year or so we may see a great piece of history in the making. You know what I refer to?'

'Curty's rocket flight, sir?' cried a shrill voice.

The schoolmaster nodded. 'Yes. Mr. Curtance is going

to try to win the Keuntz Prize for the first inter-planetary flight. Mr. Curtance, as you know, is a very brave man. A lot of poeple have already tried to win that prize, and, as far as we know, they have all died in the attempt.

'Many men lost their lives in trying to reach the Moon, and most people said it was impossible for them to do it—there was even a movement to get their attempts banned. But the men went on trying. Duncan, K. K. Smith and Sudden actually got there, but they crashed on the surface and were killed. Then came the great Drivers. In 1969 he managed to take his rocket right round the Moon and bring it safely back to Earth. Everybody was astounded, and for the first time they really began to believe that we could leave the Earth if we tried hard enough. Mr. Keuntz, who lived in Chicago, said: "If man can reach the Moon, he can reach the planets." And he put aside five million dollars to be given to the first men who should get there and back.

'The first one to try was Jornsen. His rocket was too heavy. He fell back and landed somewhere in the Pacific Ocean. Then the great Drivers tried. He got up enough speed not to fall back, like Jornsen, but he wasn't fast enough to get right away, and he stuck. His rocket is still up there; sometimes they catch a glimpse of it in the big telescopes, circling round the Earth for ever, like a tiny moon.'

'Please, sir, what happened to Drivers himself?'

'He must have starved to death, poor man—unless his air gave out first. He had a friend with him, and perhaps theirs is the worst of all the tragedies—trapped in an orbit where they could look down on the world, knowing that they would never get back.'

'After that came Simpson whose rocket was built in Keuntz's own works. He took off somewhere in Illinois, but something went wrong. It fell on the lake shore, just outside Chicago, and blew up with a terrible explosion which wrecked hundreds of houses and killed I don't know how many people.

'Since then there have been ten or more attempts.

Some have fallen back, others have got away and never been heard of since.'

'Then somebody may have done it already, without our knowing it, sir?'

'It is possible. We can't tell.'

'Do you think Curty will do it, sir?'

'One can't tell that, either. But if he does he will make a more important piece of history than did even Columbus.'

At three o'clock Mr. Jefferson, physics master in the same school, demonstrated to an interested if rather sceptical class that rocket propulsion was even more efficient in a vacuum than in air.

'Newton taught us,' he began, 'that to every action there is an equal and opposite reaction ...'

At four o'clock the news came to a bungalow half-way up the side of a Welsh mountain. The girl who brought it was breathing hard after her climb from the village below, and she addressed the middle-aged man in the bungalow's one sitting-room excitedly.

'Daddy, they're saying that Dale Curtance is going to try for the Keuntz Prize.'

'What? Let me see.'

He pounced on the copy of the *Excess* which protruded from her shopping-bag, and settled down to it with a kind of desperate avidity.

'At last,' he said, as he reached the end of the column, 'at last. Now they will find out that we were right. We shall be able to leave here, Joan. We shall be able to go back and look them in the face.'

'Perhaps, but he hasn't done it yet, Daddy.'

'Young Curtance will do it if anyone can. And they'll have to believe him.'

'But, Daddy dear, it doesn't even say that he is going to try for Mars. Venus is much nearer; it's probably that.'

'Nonsense, Joan, nonsense. Of course it's Mars. Look here, it says he intends to start sometime in October. Well, Mars comes into opposition about the middle of

24

April next year. Obviously he's working on Drivers' estimates of just under twelve weeks for the outward journey and under eleven for the return. That will give him a few days there to prospect and to overhaul his machine. He can't afford to leave the return a day past opposition. You see, it all fits in.'

'I don't see, darling, but I've no doubt you're right.'

'Of course I'm right, it's as plain as can be. I'm going to write to him.'

The girl shook her head.

'I shouldn't do that. He might hand it over to one of the newspapers—and you know what that would mean.'

The man paused in his elation, and frowned.

'Yes. Perhaps he would. We'll wait, my dear. We'll wait until he tells them what he's found there. Then we'll go back home and see who laughs last . . .'

At five o'clock a telephone conversation between Mrs. Dale Curtance and her mother-in-law was in progress.

'. . . But, Mary dear, this is useless,' the elder Mrs. Curtance was saying. 'You'll never be able to stop him. I know Dale. Once he's made his mind up to a thing like this, he can't be stopped.'

'But he must be stopped. I can't let him do it. I'll move everything to stop him. You don't know what it means to me.'

'My dear, I know what it means to me—and I am his mother. I also know something of what it means to him. We've just got to suppress our own selfishness.'

'Selfishness! You call it selfishness to try to stop him killing himself?'

'Mary, don't you see what you are doing? You're losing him. If you did manage to stop him, he'd hate you for it, and if you go on as you are doing, he'll hate you for trying to stop him. Please, please give it up, Mary. It's not fair on Dale or yourself or the child. In your condition you can't afford to behave like this. All we can do is what most women have to do—make the best of it.'

'Oh, you don't understand. Without him there'll be nothing for me to make the best of.'

'There will be the child, Mary. You must get right away from all this. Come down here and stay quietly with me till that's over.'

'How can I "stay quietly" anywhere while this is going on? You must come up and see him. Perhaps if we both talked to him—— Will you come?'

Mrs. Curtance paused before she answered.

'All right. I will come.'

She put down the receiver and sighed. The most that she could hope for was that Mary should be convinced of the futility of kicking against fate.

At six o'clock the announcer read two S.O.S. messages and the weather report, and added:

'No doubt everyone has read the newspaper reports of Mr. Curtance's proposed bid for the Keuntz Prize. We have been able to persuade Mr. Curtance himself to come to the studio to tell you what he hopes to do. Mr. Dale Curtance.'

Dale's pleasant features faded in on millions of television screens, smiling in a friendly fashion at his unseen audience.

'It is kind of the B.B.C. to invite me here this evening,' he began, 'and I am grateful to them for giving me the opportunity to correct certain misunderstandings which seem to be current regarding my intentions. Firstly, let me say that it is quite true that I mean to attempt to reach another planet and to return to Earth. And it is also true, for a number of reasons which I will not go into now, that the planet I have chosen for this attempt is Mars. But it is quite untrue that I intend to make this flight alone. Actually there will be five of us aboard my ship when she takes off.

'I should like to dispel, too, the prevalent idea that I am engaged in deliberate suicide. I assure you we are not. All five of us could easily find much cheaper and less arduous ways of killing ourselves.

'There are, of course, risks. In fact, there are three distinct kinds of risk: the known ones which we can and shall prepare against: the known ones which we must trust to luck to avoid: and the entirely unknown. *But* we are convinced that we have more than a sporting chance against them all—if we were not, we should not be making the attempt.

'Thanks to the courage and pertinacity of those who from the time of Piccard's ascent into the stratosphere in 1931 have pushed forward the examination of space, we shall not be shooting ourselves into the completely unknown. Thanks also to them, the design of my ship will be an improvement on any which has gone before, and unlike those of the early pioneers she is designed to contend with many of the known conditions of space as well as in the hope of surviving the unknown. Each expedition to leave Earth stands a better chance of success than its predecessor—which is another way of saying that it risks less. Therefore, I say that if we are successful in this venture, if we gain for Britain the honour of being the first nation to achieve trans-spatial communication, it must never be forgotten that better men than we gave their lives to make it possible.

'If one can single out one man from an army of heroes and say, "This is the greatest of them all," I should point my finger at Richard Drivers. Compared with the risks that brave genius took, we take none. The story of that amazing man's persistence in the face of a jeering world when three of his friends had already crashed to their deaths upon the Moon, and the tale of his lonely flight around it are among the deathless epics of the race. Whatever may be done by us or by others after us, his achievement stands alone. And it will be he who made the rest possible.

'So, you see, we are not pioneers. We are only followers in a great tradition, hoping to tread the way of knowledge a little farther than the last man. If it is granted to us to be successful, we shall be satisfied to have been not entirely unworthy of our forerunners and of our country.'

The red light flickered and the televising mechanism slowed as the studio was cut off from the world. An important looking gentleman entered. He greeted Dale and shook hands.

'Thank you,' he said. 'Very good of you to come at such short notice.'

Dale grinned and shook his head. 'No, my thanks are due to you.' The other looked puzzled. 'You've not seen this evening's *Banner*?' Dale went on. 'They're trying to stop me. That means the *Hail* will be at it tomorrow. I was glad to get my word in first.'

'Trying to stop you?'

'Yes. Don't know why. Some stunt of theirs, I suppose. Nobody's going to stop me, but they might be a bit of nuisance if they got a big following.'

'H'm. It's a wonder people don't get sick of Dithernear's stunts, but they don't seem to. Well, I'm glad you came—and I hope you are as optimistic as you sounded.'

'I am—nearly,' Dale admitted, as they parted.

CHAPTER IV

AND REACTIONS

INTO the Curtance sheds where the great rocket rested in its thicket of scaffolding only the faintest ripples of popular excitement penetrated. Though Dale gave interviews freely enough to avid pressmen, he was adamant in his refusal to permit interruption in the routine of his shops, and the reception of those few journalists who attempted to enter by subterfuge was ungentle. An augmented corps of watchmen with the assistance of police dogs guarded doors behind which work went on with the same unhurried efficiency as in the days before the secret was out. The most obvious and concrete result of world-wide interest was a new shed hastily run up to accommodate Dale's swollen secretariat.

The inquest upon the intruder was reported in full detail and followed with close attention, but it failed to provide any sensational revelations, and the body remained unidentified. The chief witness gave his evidence clearly, received the congratulations of the coroner upon his narrow escape and left the court with an increased reputation for courage.

Two days later the *Chicago Emblem* announced that the dead man had been an American citizen named Forder. It indignantly demanded a closer inquiry into the circumstances, hinting that Dale might show up less well. The leader on the subject finished by truculently demanding the passage of a special bill through Congress to prevent the Keuntz Prize from going abroad.

'That's the point,' Fuller said as he showed the article to Dale. 'That's the Keuntz works behind this, I'll bet. They're afraid of you lifting the prize.'

Dale nodded. 'Looks like it. Still, it's good news in one way. It suggests that they aren't building a rocket to try for it themselves.'

'I don't know.' Fuller was less sanguine. 'I know our reports say so, but you never can tell how much double and triple crossing is going on with these agents. It might equally well mean that they are having a shot at it and think that any rivals will be put off if there is no chance of their getting the prize.'

'Well, our men haven't let us down yet. You can be sure that if they were building a space rocket anywhere we'd have heard of it somehow—just as they or somebody else seem to have heard of ours.'

'Perhaps. I should say it was they, since the man you shot was an American. Anyway, they're out to get that prize—and the interest it's accumulated. Apart from the money, it'd put them back at the top of the rocket-plane industry. Their reputation's been slumping badly the last year or two, you know—for anyone else to get it would mean the end of them.'

The following day the *Daily Hail* threw overboard its noisy but uninfectious policy of Save Britain's Speed King From Himself and joined with the *Excess* in a vituperative duet against the *Emblem*. A scathing reply from the latter involving George III and the American debt was side-tracked by the *Potsdamer Tageblatt* which pointed out on behalf of the Fatherland that Keuntz, a German before he was an American, had with true

German generosity offered his prize to the whole world. Keuntz, replied the *Emblem*, with some heat, was also a Jew who had been forced to flee from the kindly Fatherland in the days of the first Führer. America, the land of the free, had given him sanctuary, therefore, etc., etc. And the battle went on.

Outside the main brawl the *Views-Record* was announcing that 'Mars Must be Internationalized'. Swannen Haffer in the *Daily Socialist* was asking, 'Will the Martian Workers be Exploited?' The *Daily Artisan* was predicting the discovery of a flourishing system of Martian Soviets. Gerald Birdy wrote articles on 'Planning a New World' and the need for a Planetician in the Cabinet. *Woman's Love* in publishing an article on 'Wives of Pioneers' with special, if inaccurate, references to Mary Curtance (who, though journalistically unfortunate in lacking children of her own, was indiscriminately devoted to those of other people), narrowly missed making the one scoop of its life. The *Illustrated London Views* published a sectional drawing of a typical rocket-ship and gave interesting data on the solar system. The *Wexford Bee-Keepers' Gazette* announced that it had its eye on Mr. Curtance, and warned him to stay where God had put him.

The shares of Commercial Explosives, Limited, rose for three days as if propelled by their own fuel, and then fell back to a little above normal. A heavy slump in the price of gold took everyone by surprise. The cause was traced to a rumour that spectroscopy showed the presence of gold in great quantities on Mars; the rumour was duly exploded, but gold failed to respond. This caused less surprise, the behaviour of gold being unaccountable at the best of times. The Stock Exchange betting stood at 500 to one against Dale reaching Mars, and 10,000 to one against the double journey. A rumour that the Russians had for years been building a bigger and better rocket, to be called the *Tovaritch*, refused to be crushed until the Soviet Government issued an official denial of such a rocket's existence or even contemplation. Rumours of German, American and Japanese rival rockets were less hardy. The pastime of guessing the names of Dale's companions attained the status of a national game.

Meanwhile the work on the Curtance rocket went steadily forward throughout the summer. Dale was too busy to feel anything save an anxiety that his ship should be finished to schedule by the middle of September—certainly too busy to feel lonely because his wife had gone to his mother's home.

For Mary had given in. She had dropped her opposition and released him from his promise, but she had been unable to stand the sense of restlessness pervading the house. She had fled to the quiet Dorset countryside where only an occasional gyrocurt with its white sails whirling as it sauntered along amid summer clouds reminded her of the reign of machines.

Occasionally the child moved in her womb, hurting her. It would not be long now. Poor baby, what a world to come into. She hoped it would be a boy. This was a man's world, women walked unhappily and fearfully among its gears and flywheels, making shift with dreams and snatching what little joy was spared them. The machines were the hateful dictators of men and women alike. Only men could be so dense as to think that they themselves were the rulers . .

CHAPTER V

GREAT DAY

THE few hardy souls who had elected to spend the night upon the open inhospitality of Salisbury Plain slept no later than dawn upon the morning of the twelfth of October, 1981, for it was with the first rays of sunlight that the influx which would last all day began.

The hysterical ballyhoo timed to reach its climax upon this day had been sustained with an unsurpassed degree of journalistic art. The birth of a son to Dale Curtance had given a fillip to interest at a convenient

31

moment, and every newspaper reader in the country had become familiar with the, at present, somewhat dough-like features of Victor Curtance. The announcement of the names of Dale's companions for the flight had caught three unknown men and one rather more familiar figure into an undying fulguration of publicity. Every person who could reach a radio set had seen and heard a prince of the royal blood say: 'I name this ship the *Gloria Mundi*. May God guide her and bring her safely back to us,' and the film of the occasion had been shown at every cinema. The arduous feat of transporting the *Gloria Mundi* from the sheds of her birth at Kingston to a suitably desolate portion of Salisbury Plain for the take off, had been followed in detail with critical attention. The discovery by an advance guard that a part of the route had been tampered with and the subsequent disinterment of a case of dynamite (with detonator and wires attached) had roused indignation and speculation to feverish heats. The assurance that Dale himself was continually guarded by two or more armed police detectives met with immense popular appreciation. The song, 'Curty, the King of the Clouds', written at the time of the first Equatorial Flight, had been revived and stood in frequency of performance second only to the National Anthem. For the last fortnight the Press had really let itself go, and in loyal response to its efforts the public was prepared to invade the Plain on a scale pertubing to the authorities.

The first active sign of preparation in the grey light of that historic Monday was the ascent of more than a dozen small captive balloons, painted a bright yellow, and ranged in a circle about the scene of operations. Within the perimeter they marked no craft save police patrols was to be permitted at any height whatever, and it was considered likely that the five-mile circle would insure an ample margin of safety. Half a dozen police gyrocurts rose and set themselves to hover in positions strategic for the control of traffic both by land and air. The first great charaplane of the day came booming out of the west. It landed to deposit its passengers, and within five minutes had taken off again to fetch another load. Machines of every kind from the dainty flipabout to the massive gyrobus, all with the early morning sunlight glancing from brightly painted bodies beneath swirling white sails, started to float in from each quarter, and the task of directing them to their appointed parks began in earnest. Within half an hour of the first car's arrival the congested road traffic had slowed to a tedious, bottom-gear crawl.

The crowds began to pour from the 'plane-parks and car-parks, making for their enclosures and, the favoured few, for the stands. Hawkers in good voice offered silver trinkets in the form of miniature rockets, picture postcards of Dale, pictures of the rocket-ship itself and printed handkerchiefs as suitable mementoes of the occasion. A hundred camp-kitchens began to cater for the hungry. Half a dozen loudspeakers burst into the inevitable 'Curty, the King of the Clouds'. A number of persons were already failing to Find the Lady. And still it was only eight a.m.

Somewhere about nine-thirty Police Gyrocurt Number 4 came hovering close to Number 5. Number 4's pilot picked up a megaphone and shouted across:

'Just look at 'em down there. Bill. Like a bloomin' ant-'eap, ain't it?'

Bill, in Number 5, nodded.

'If they keep on comin' in at this rate, we'll 'ave to start parking them vertical,' he bawled back.

That part of the Plain which lay below them had undergone a transformation. Outside the five-mile circle of the beacon balloons acres of country were covered with parked cars and 'planes. From them crowds of black dots were stippled inwards, growing denser as they converged. The barrier which held the public back out of harm's way appeared already as a solid black ring two miles in diameter and of greater thickness on the western side where the several stands, broadcasting and observation towers and various other temporary structures were situated. Finally, in splendid isolation in the exact centre, could be seen the *Gloria Mundi* herself.

The portable sheds of those who had attended to the last tests and adjustments had been cleared away leaving only discoloured rectangles of grass to show where they had stood for the last fortnight. Gone also was the galvanized-iron fence which had served to keep back the curious during that time, and the rocket, still shrouded in canvas, was left with a cordon of police as her only guard.

By midday the crowd was still swelling. The refreshment stalls were beginning to wonder whether the supply would hold out, and in accordance with economic laws were raising their prices. A self-appointed prophet beneath a banner, consenting that 'God's Will be Done', patiently warned a regrettably waggish audience of the sacrilegious aspect of the occasion. Up on the broadcast tower an announcer told the world, confidently:

'It's a beautiful day. Couldn't be better for it. The crowds are still coming in as they have been all day, and although the take-off is timed for half-past four, the excitement is already tremendous. I expect you can hear the noise they are making out there. There must be over half a million people here now. Don't you think so, Mr. Jones?'

Mr. Jones was understood to suggest three-quarters of a million as the minimum.

'Perhaps you're right. At any rate there are a lot of them, and it really is a beautiful day. Don't you think so, Mr. Jones?'

Rumours flocked to the Press Stand and to the rooms beneath it like iron filings to a magnet.

'Her tubes won't stand it,' said Travers of the *Hail*. 'Man I know, metallurgist in Sheffield, told me for a fact that there is no alloy known which will stand up to such a temperature——'

'She can't rise,' Dennis of the *Reflector* was saying. 'She's too heavy. Man in Commercial Explosives showed me the figures. She'll turn over and streak along the ground—and I hope to God she doesn't come my way——'

'If she gets up,' conceded Dawes of *Veracity*, 'she's not

got a chance in hell of getting out of the gravity pull. Take my word for it, it's going to be another Drivers business——'

Tenson of the *Co-ordinator* knew for a fact that the drive for the rapid construction had meant incomplete testing.

'Sheer madness,' was the *Excess* man's view. 'Rockets have got to be small. Might as well try to fly St. Paul's as take up this great thing——'

A small, insignificant member of the crowd plucked at Police Sergeant Yarder's sleeve and pointed upwards.

'Look, Officer, there's a gyrocurt inside the beacons.'

Sergeant Yarder shaded his eyes and followed the line of the pointing finger.

'That'll be Mr. Curtance and the rest, sir. Got to let *them* through, or there wouldn't be no show.'

Others had noticed the 'plane's arrival. A sound of cheering rose, faint at first, but growing in volume until it swept up in a great roar from tens of thousands of throats as more and more of the spectators realized that Dale was here at last. The 'plane dropped slowly and landed. The door opened and Dale could be seen waving in reply. He stepped to the ground and his four chosen companions followed. A few moments later they were all hidden from the crowd by a converging rush of movie-vans and Press-cars. The gyrocurt took off again and the mob of vans and cars moved closer to the still-shrouded rocket.

The announcer up in the broadcasting tower talked excitedly into his microphone:

'He's here! You have just seen Dale Curtance arrive to make his inter-planetary attempt. They're moving over now towards the rocket. The five are somewhere in the middle of that group there. The crowd is shouting itself hoarse. Here, we are more than a mile from the rocket itself, but we are going to do our best to show you the unveiling ceremony. Just a minute, please, while we change the lens.'

The scene on the vision screens flickered and then

35

blurred as the teleoptic was swung in. It refocused, searched, and finally came to rest on Dale and the group about him. He stood on a temporary wooden dais at the rocket's foot. In one hand he held the end of a rope which ran upwards out of television screen's field.

'Now we are going over to hear Mr. Curtance himself speak through the microphone which you can see beside him,' said the announcer.

A sudden, expectant silence fell on the crowds. Those who had brought portable screens with them watched Dale step forward smiling. The rest shaded their eyes to gaze at the group a mile away and imagine that well-known smile as a hundred loudspeakers spoke at once:

'Anything I could say in answer to such a salute as you have given me must be inadequate. All that I can say, on behalf of my companions and myself, is "Thank you". We are going to do our best to prove ourselves worthy of such a reception. Again, "Thank you".'

He paused and tightened his hold on the hanging rope.

'And now,' he added, 'here is my *Gloria Mundi*.'

He pulled on the rope. For a breathless second nothing seemed to happen. Then the canvas fell away from the top, slithering down the polished metal sides to subside in billowing waves on the ground. The earlier cheers had been but a murmur compared with the volume of sound which now roared from the packed crowds.

The *Gloria Mundi* gleamed in the sunlight. She towered on the level plain like a monstrous shell designed for the artillery of giants; a shapely mass of glistening metal poised on a tripod of three great flanges, her blunt nose pointing already into the blue sky whither—if all went well—she would presently leap.

And then, surprisingly, the cheering died away. It was as though it had come home to the mass of sightseers for the first time that the five men on the platform were volunteers for almost certain death; that the shell-like shape beside them was indeed a shell—the greatest projectile the world had ever seen, and that all of it, save for a small part near the nose where the circular windows showed, was filled with the most powerful known explosives.

When the crowd began to talk again a new note was dominant. The spirit of bank holiday jubilation had become inpregnated with anxiety and a sense of trepidation. Even the phlegmatic Sergeant Yarder was aware of its injection.

The proposed flight had hitherto stirred his imagination only slightly; and that because the crowd attending its start was the largest on record. Now he looked across at the rocket with a new curiosity. Why wasn't the Earth big enough for them? It must be a queer kind of man who could find so little of interest in all the five continents and seven seas that he wished to shoot himself out into the emptiness of space. And what good would it do anybody, even if they managed it? What good had any of these rockets ever done? Even Drivers' flight round the Moon hadn't meant anybody's betterment. There had been millions of money wasted and scores of good men killed . . .

The sergeant sniffed and pulled out his watch. It was useful, though not an instrument of precision.

'Just gone 'alf-past three. They got an hour yet,' he murmured, half to himself.

His small neighbour ventured a correction.

'Twenty to four, I think, Sergeant. They'll be going inside soon.'

The sergeant shook a disapproving head.

'Why do they do it? Blamed if I'd ever go up in one of them things—not for millions, I wouldn't. Bein' a national 'ero's all right—but it ain't much good to you if you're all in little bits so small that nobody can find 'em—— And it ain't no good if you go the way Drivers did, poor devil.'

'I don't think Curtance will do that'—the other shook his head. 'He's a great man, and this *Gloria Mundi* of his is the greatest ship yet. He ought to do it.'

'Suppose it blows up?' asked the sergeant.

The small man smiled. 'We shan't know much about

that, I think.'

The sergeant moved uneasily. 'But it can't 'urt us 'ere, can it? Look at the distance.'

'But the distance is only to keep us out of the way of the exhausts. If the *Gloria Mundi* should blow up—well, remember Simpson at Chicago; his rocket was only half the size of this.'

For a few silent moments the sergeant remembered Simpson uncomfortably.

'But what do they want to do it for?' he inquired again, plaintively.

The other shrugged his shoulders. 'It seems not so much that they want to as that they must, I think. Something seems to drive them on and on whether they want it or not.'

The small circular door high up in the rocket's side shut with a decisive thud. The few favoured pressmen who had been allowed upon the small staging beside it clattered down the wooden steps and joined their less privileged fellows on the ground. Almost before the last of them was clear a squad of workmen was tipping over staging and steps together to load them across a lorry. The movie-vans and the journalists' cars began to jolt over the grass towards the Press enclosure. Not far behind them followed the trucks carrying the last of the workmen. The *Gloria Mundi*, glowing in the rays of the sinking sun, was left sheer and solitary.

Barnes, of the *Daily Photo*, looked back at her with resentment.

'No appeal,' he grumbled. 'No woman's angle. That's the trouble about this job. Damn it all, it's a wife's duty to show up at a time like this—*and* to bring the kid. The public wants to see pictures of the final embrace—it's got a right to. Instead of that, his wife sits at home and watches it all over the radio. Can you beat it? It's not fair on us—nor on the public. If I were him, I'd damn' well see that my wife——'

'Oh, shut up,' said his neighbour. 'What the hell do your people run an art department for if it isn't to do a bit of *montage* at times like this. You have a look at our

38

picture of the last farewell tomorrow. It's good. Nearly brought tears to my eyes when I first saw it last week.'

The cars ran into the enclosure. Their freight disembarked and made for the bar. Once more the loudspeakers burst out with 'Curty, the King of the Clouds'. The minute-hands of thousands of watches passed the figure twelve and began to loiter down the final half-hour.

CHAPTER VI

THE START

'TWENTY minutes,' said Dale, unemotionally.

If the others heard him, they gave no sign of it. He looked at them, noticing their reactions to the strain of waiting as they stood clustered close to the circular windows. Of the five men in the steel room he was the least affected. His years of rocket racing had bred in him the ability to face the start of an adventure in a spirit of cold fatalism—or, perhaps more accurately, to anaesthetize temporarily his natural emotions. The other four were gazing through the thick-fused quartz panes across the unlovely Plain as though it were the most beautiful view on Earth.

Geoffrey Dugan, the youngest of them, took the least trouble to hide his feelings. Dale looked sympathetically at his eyes shining brightly with excitement, noted his parted lips and quick breathing through closed teeth. He knew just what Dugan was feeling. Had he not gone through it all himself? He had been twenty-four, just Dugan's present age, when he had flown in the Equatorial race, and he had not forgotten his sensations before the start. The lad was the right stuff. He was glad that he had chosen him out of the thousands of possibles to be his assistant pilot and navigator.

Froud, the journalist, turned and caught his eye, grinned unconvincingly, and then looked back to the window. Dale noticed that he was fidgeting. So the tension was getting under that cynical gentleman's skin, was it?

James Burns, the engineer, leaned against the glass, looking out. To appearance he was almost as calm as Dale himself, but when he moved, it was with a tell-tale, irritable jerk. The expression on his face maintained a proper solemnity as would become one about to attend his own funeral.

As far as his crew was concerned Dale's only misgivings were on account of its last member. The sight of the doctor's face, ominously white and haggard, worried him. There had been much criticism of his decision to include this man of fifty-six in his party, and it began to look as if the critics might be justified. Still, it was too late now for regrets—one could only hope for the best.

Doctor Grayson lifted his eyes to the clear blue sky and gave an involuntary shudder. His face felt clammy and he knew that it was pale. He knew, too, that his eyes were looking glassy behind his thick spectacle lenses and his utmost efforts could not altogether restrain the trembling of his hands. Moreover, his imagination was persistently perverse. It continually showed him pictures of city streets filled with crowds, noisy with rumbling traffic, brilliant with lights of all colours, blinking and twinkling. It repeatedly told him that if he had the sense to get out of this steel room, he could be in such a place this very night ...

Froud looked across the Plain to the black line held in check by an army of police. Up on the Press tower were the small, dark figures of men he knew, fellow journalists to whom he had said good-bye a short while ago. They had all professed envy of him. He doubted whether one of them meant it or would have been willing to change places with him, given the chance. At the moment he himself would willingly have changed places with any one of them. He turned to look again at the closely packed crowds.

'Thousands and thousands of them, all waiting for the big bang,' he murmured. 'They'll probably get a bigger earful than they want—— Hullo, there's someone with a heliograph.' He leaned forward, causing the characteristic sickle-shaped lock of black hair to fall across his forehead.

'G-O-O-D L-U-C-K,' he spelt out from the flashes. 'Hardly original, but kindly meant—and that's better than a lot of them. I wouldn't mind betting that there's a whole crowd out there—not excluding my professional brethren—who'd consider it a better show if we blew up than if we went up.'

'Aye, you're right there,' agreed Burns, his deep voice according well with his gloomy expression. 'They're the kind who don't feel they've had their money's worth unless some poor body crashes in an air race. But they're going to be disappointed with the *Gloria Mundi*. I helped to build her, and she's not going to blow up.'

The doctor moved, irritably.

'I wish you two wouldn't talk about blowing up. Isn't this waiting bad enough without imagining horrors?'

Young Geoffrey Dugan agreed with him. His look of eager anticipation was becoming supplanted by a worried frown.

'I'm with you, Doc. I wish we could get going now. This hanging about's getting me down. How much longer?' he added, turning back to Dale.

'Quarter of an hour,' Dale told him. 'We better be getting ready, Dugan. What's it say on the weather tower?'

Dugan crossed to one of the other windows.

'Wind speed twelve miles an hour,' he said.

'Good. Not much allowance necessary for that.' Dale turned back to the others. 'Put up the shutters now. It's time we got to the hammocks.'

He switched on a small light set in the ceiling. The shutter-plates, heavy pieces of steel alloy, were swung across and their rubber-faced edges clamped into place. When the last had been screwed down to its utmost and made airtight, the men turned to their hammocks.

These were couches slung by metal rods. Finely tempered steel and softest down had been used in an effort to produce the acme of comfort. No fairy-tale princess ever rested upon a bed one-half so luxuriously yielding as those provided for the five men.

They climbed on to them without speaking, and felt for the safety-straps. The doctor's pale face had gone yet whiter. Little beads of sweat were gathering beneath his lower lip. Dugan saw him fumbling clumsily with the straps, and leaned across.

'Here, let me do it, Doc,' he suggested.

The doctor nodded his thanks and lay back while Dugan's strong, steady hands slid the webbing into the buckles.

'Five minutes,' said Dale.

Dugan attended to his own straps, then all five lay waiting.

The engineer rested motionless with all the graven solemnity of a stone knight upon his tomb. The journalist wriggled slightly to find the most comfortable position.

'Good beds you give your guests, Dale,' he murmured. 'Makes one wonder why we're such damn' fools as ever to do anything but sleep.'

Dale lay silent, his eyes fixed upon a flicking second-hand. The fingers of his right hand already grasped the starting-lever set into the side of his couch. His concentration left him without visible sign of fear, excitement or worry.

'Two minutes.'

The tension increased. Froud ceased to fidget. Dugan felt his heart begin to beat more quickly. The doctor started to count the seconds subconsciously; the surface of his mind was tormented with suggestions. Even yet it was not too late. If he were to jump up and attack Dale . . .

'Half a minute.'

'And then—what?' thought the doctor. He turned his head. His uneasy eyes met Dugan's, and he heard a murmur of encouragement.

'Fifteen seconds,' said Dale.

A comforting fatalism crept over the doctor. One must die sooner or later. Why not now? He'd had a good run for his money. If only it were quick . . .

'Five—four—three—two—one . . .'

The chattering of the crowd died down to a murmur, and thence to an excited silence broken only by the voice from the loudspeakers inexorably counting away the time. Every eye was turned to the centre of the circle, each focused upon the glittering rocket, scarcely daring even to blink lest it should miss the critical moment of the start. Into the dullest mind there crept at this moment some understanding of the scene's true meaning—a thrill of pride in the indomitable spirit of man striving once again to break his age-old bondage: reaching out to grasp the very stars.

So, into unknown perils had gone the galleys of Ericson; so, too, had gone the caravels of Columbus, fearing that they might sail over the edge of the world into the Pit of Eternity, but persistent in their courage. It might well be that this day, this twelfth of October, 1981, would go down to history as a turning-point in human existence—it might well be . . .

The telescopes in the great observatories were trained and ready. They had been trained before. They had followed the flaring tracks of adventurers from Earth, had seen them break from the shell of atmosphere into the emptiness of space, seen them fail to hold their courses and watched the beginnings of falls which would last for months until they should end at last in the sun. And now, before long, the fate of the *Gloria Mundi* would be told by the great lenses—whether fate had decided that she should turn aside to be drawn relentlessly into the centre of the system, or whether she would be allowed to see the red disc of Mars growing slowly larger in the sky before her . . .

The last tense seconds passed. The watchers held their breath and strained their eyes.

A flash stabbed out between the tail fins. The great rocket lifted. She seemed balanced upon a point of fire, soaring like the huge shell she was into the blue above. Fire spewed from her ports in a spreading glory of livid flame like the tail of a monstrous comet. And when the thunder of her going beat upon the ears of the crowd, she was already a fiery spark in the heavens. . . .

The *Daily Hail*'s correspondent had left his telephone on the Press tower and was gravitating naturally towards the bar. Before he could reach it, he found himself accosted by an excited individual clad in mechanic's overalls. This person gripped him firmly by the lapel.

'Mr. Travers, do you want a scoop?' he inquired urgently.

Travers detached the none too clean hand.

'Scoop?' he said. 'There are no scoops nowadays. Everybody knows all about everything before it's happened.'

'Don't you believe it,' the mechanic insisted earnestly. 'I've got a real scoop for you if you see that I'm treated right.'

'The *Hail* always treats everybody right,' Travers said loyally. 'What is it? About the rocket?'

The mechanic nodded. After a hasty glance to reassure himself that no one else was within hearing, he leaned closer and whispered in the journalist's ear. Travers stopped him after the first sentence.

'Nobody else knows?'

'Not a soul. Take my oath on it.'

Two minutes later, the mechanic, with Travers firmly clasping his arm, was being rushed across the ground in the direction of the *Hail*'s special 'plane.

CHAPTER VII

IN FLIGHT

DOCTOR GRAYSON'S eyes were tightly shut. The lids were pressed desperately together as though the slender membranes could cut him off from all sensation. Dugan's were open, and his head was turned slightly to one side as he watched Dale. The control-lever and the hand upon it were hidden from him, but he could see the right arm stiffen as Dale's fingers gripped.

There was a sudden roar, loud and terrifying in spite of the evacuated double walls. An invisible weight pressed him deep into the cushions of his couch. The shuddering of the rocket shook him all over, despite the intervening springs, with a vibration which seemed to be shaking him to pieces. His head was swimming, and his brains felt like lead in his skull.

A new high note, a penetrating shriek, soared above the roar as the atmosphere fled screaming past outside. With an effort he managed to turn his head and look at the thermometer suspended above Dale. The temperature of the outer hull was rising already, and the speed indicator was only yet moving past the mile a second mark—three thousand, six hundred miles an hour—Dugan was swept by a sudden panic—did Dale know?

Dale's eyes were fixed on the large disc which bore only a single second-hand. Slowly, and in accordance with the planned acceleration of a hundred feet per second, per second, he was turning the control lever. And slowly the speed indicator was advancing. Intangible forces continued to press on the men. It became difficult to breathe. The fine springs and soft down felt like cast iron: compressed internal organs ached intolerably; hearts laboured: veins rose in cords. Heads burned and drummed: eyes no longer seemed to fit their sockets.

The whine of the air passed beyond hearing; the thermometer continued to rise, but it was still far below the red danger-mark. The speed indicator slid forward —three and a half—four—four and a half miles a second—four minutes since the start . . . A little behind schedule . . .

Dugan ceased to watch. He could no longer see clearly. His eyes felt as though they must burst. Like a refrain in his mind went the repetition: 'Seven miles a second . . . Seven miles a second . . .' Less than that would mean failure to get free from Earth.

The pressure grew. Dale was increasing the acceleration beyond the hundred feet. The weight ground down on the men, crushing them with an intolerable agony, straining ribs as though to crack them ... At last Dugan slipped into unconsciousness ...

Dugan, the youngest and the strongest, was the first to open his eyes. He was immediately and violently sick. Before he had completely recovered the others were beginning to stir and to show similar symptoms. His first anxiety when he gained a little control of himself was the speed indicator, and he sighed with relief to see that it was registering a trifle above seven miles a second— actually a point or two beneath seven might not have failed to tear them free from Earth's attraction, but the safety-margin would have been unpleasantly narrow. He turned over on his side to look at Dale who had begun to move slightly. How the man had held out against the pressure to accelerate to such a point was a mystery. Somebody, Dugan decided, would have to invent an automatic acceleration control.

He sat up with great caution and released his straps. The rocket tubes were shut off now, and the ship travelling under her own momentum, so there would be no appreciable pull of gravity. He unfastened a pair of magnetic soled shoes from their holders beside his couch and strapped them on before lowering his feet to the floor.

Burns was less circumspect. He undid his buckles, sat up abruptly and met the ceiling with a smack. He swore.

'Why don't you use your brains?' the doctor grumbled, peevishly. He was feeling extremely unwell and remained quite unamused by the spectacle of Dugan dragging the engineer back to his couch.

'I didn't think we were going to hit the no-gravity zone so soon,' Burns explained. The doctor shook his head.

'There's no such thing as no gravity,' he told him severely.

'Is there not, now? Well, it feels as if there is, blast it,' said the other ungratefully.

'Don't let Doc bother you,' advised Froud, pausing in the act of reaching for his shoes. 'You were quite in the best tradition. Wells' and Verne's people biffed about just like that. I say, can't we open one of those shutters?'

Dugan looked at the still horizontal Dale.

'Better wait for orders.'

'That's all right.' Dale's voice came weakly. 'Go ahead —if the windows aren't broken. I'll lie here a bit.'

The three began to tackle one of the shutters while the doctor searched in his case for a syringe before moving over to Dale. There was some difficulty in unscrewing the shutters. With no weight in their bodies to act as leverage every movement required purchase in the opposite direction, but at length the shutter was made to swing back.

Stars like diamonds, bright and undiffused, shone in brilliant myriads against a velvet blackness. Bright sparks which were great suns burnt lonely, with nothing to illuminate in a darkness they could not dissipate. In the empty depths of space there was no size, no scale, nothing to show that a million light years was not arm's length, or arm's length, a million light years. Microcosm was confused with macrocosm.

For a short time no one spoke, then:

'Where's the Earth?' Froud asked.

'She'll rise soon. We're twisting slightly,' Dugan told him.

They waited while the flaring stars slipped slowly sideways. A dark segment began to encroach, blotting everything else from sight. It swung farther and farther across their sky until upon its far edge, seemingly above them, gleamed the crescent Earth. Froud murmured half to himself: 'My God, isn't she a beauty? Shimmering like a pearl.'

The vast crescent had not the hard, clear outline of the moon. A cool, green-blue light flooded out from it as it hung huge and lucent in the sky, softened as though by a powdering of some celestial bloom.

Sunset had just overtaken Europe and the nightline was moving out on to the Atlantic. The Americas showed their zig-zag close to the outer edge, and the greater ranges of their mountains were still just discernible. It was strange to think that high in those mountains were observatories where even now telescopes were trained upon them. Still more odd to think of all the millions of men swarming with all their unimportant importance upon that beautiful piece of cosmic decay . . .

Dale and the doctor moved across and joined them. The rocket was still twisting, carrying the Earth out of sight. A sudden glare from the window took them all by surprise.

'Shut it quick, or we'll all be cooked,' ordered Dale.

The sun had 'risen' as a mass of naked, flaring flames; its heat was intense, and its brilliance too vivid to be suffered. Dugan and Burns together slammed the shutter across.

Dale turned and made his way to the control seat where he began to study the dials and gauges. The maximum thermometer showed that the acceleration had been controlled well below the danger-point. The air-pressure and condition meters read as he had expected. The speed dial, of course, remained steady at just over seven miles a second. Not until he came to the fuel-level register did he find any great deviation from his expectations, but in front of that dial he paused, frowning. There was an appreciable difference between the estimate he had made and the reading it gave. He was puzzled.

'That's queer,' he murmured to Dugan, beside him.

'It's not a great error—besides, we've gone over the seven a second mark,' said the other.

'I know, but, allowing for that, it's wrong. It's one of the simplest calculations of the lot—the amount of power required to raise a given weight at a given speed its elementary. We can't have gone wrong over that— Half a minute.'

He took a slide rule from a drawer and did some rapid calculation.

'Somewhere between a hundred and thirty and a hundred and forty pounds, I make it. Now how the hell

48

can we have gained that, I wonder?'

'You pushed up the acceleration during the fifth minute.'

'I know. I've compensated for that.' He spoke to the rest. 'Has any one of you brought anything extra aboard?'

Froud and Burns shook their heads. Their possessions had been weighed to an ounce. Doctor Grayson looked a trifle sheepish.

'Well?' Dale snapped.

'Er—my small grand-daughter, you know. She insisted that I must have a mascot.' He fumbled in a pocket and produced a cat made of black velvet. It wore a bushy tail and an arrogant expression.

Dale smiled. 'Probable weight, one ounce. We'll forgive you that, Doc. But you didn't bring, for instance, that microscope of yours?'

'No, unfortunately. You ought to have let me have that, you know, Dale. It might have been very valuable to us.'

'So might a whole lot of things, but we've had to do without them. Are the rest of you absolutely sure that you've nothing extra?'

They all shook their heads.

'Well, it's an odd point, but apart from that, everything has gone like clockwork.'

'If you had my inside, you couldn't say that,' Froud observed. 'I ache, not only all over, but all through. I've got serious doubts whether my stomach will ever expand again, and the very thought of food . . .' He pulled an expressive face.

'What's next?' Dugan asked of Dale.

'Correct our course, and stop this twisting. Couches everyone.'

Froud groaned. 'Oh, my God. Again?'

'It's nothing much this time, but it might throw you about a bit.'

For twenty minutes he and Dugan in the control seats corrected and recorrected in a series of jerks.

'That's all for the present,' Dale said, at length. 'You

can get up now, and if you want to open a shutter, that's the shady side, over there.' Turning to Dugan, he added: 'Get me charts one, two and three and we'll mark the course in detail.'

Dugan left the room by a trap-door in the floor. Beyond extended a metal ladder. The ladder could not be said to lead down, for there was now neither 'up' nor 'down' within the rocket, but it offered its rungs for the purpose of towing oneself along. The living- and control-room of the *Gloria Mundi* was situated forward, in the nose. Its floor was circular, and the walls, by reason of the projectile shape, converged slightly towards the ceiling. Dale had decided that a separate navigation-room was unnecessary. Rocket flight, once the gravitation of Earth has been offset, is not, strictly speaking, a flight at all, but a fall. When in free space and on the correct course, the only attention required is that of slight modifications by short bursts on the steering-tubes. Since it would be theoretically possible for the ship to keep her calculated track without any correction until she was slowed for landing, he considered that the provision of a special navigation cabin would be a waste of space.

Round the walls of the main room the five shuttered windows were set at equal intervals. Between them, and capable of operation when the shutters must be closed, were mounted telescopic instruments ingeniously made to pierce the double hull. Now that a radius of movement was no longer necessary, the five slung couches could be packed more closely together, a table with a magnetized surface screwed to the floor and other adaptations made for the sake of comfort during a fall which must last almost twelve weeks.

Beyond the trap-door were the store-rooms for food and other necessities. Batteries for lighting and heating. The air supply and purification plant. A small cabin, little more than a cupboard, for use in emergency as a sick-bay. A work-bench, a small light lathe and rack of tools for minor repairs, and even a corner fitted as a galley—though the anticipated difficulties of weightless cooking precluded hope of many hot meals.

With this second level, the habitable portion of the rocket ended. Beyond lay the fuel tanks with their tons of explosives, the mixing chambers and the pumps supplying the combustion chambers whence the expanding gases would roar from the driving-tubes.

Dugan towed himself towards that part of the storeroom where the charts were kept. He pushed off and floated towards the floor; his magnetized soles met it with a slight click, and immediately he began to feel more normal. Although one had expected it, there was a slight sense of uncanniness attending a weightless condition. He bent down, pulled open the long front of the chart locker, and then stood staring. When he had last seen them the charts had been neatly rolled into cylinders; now most of them had been flattened out by the pressure of acceleration. That caused him no surprise: what did, was the unmistakable toe of a boot protruding from between the folds of paper.

There was a short interval of stupefaction before he regained presence of mind enough to relatch the locker and go in search of a pistol. Back in the living-room he reported:

'There's a stowaway aboard, Dale.'

The four stared at him as the remark sank in. Dale grunted, scornfully:

'Impossible. The ship's been guarded all the time.'

'But there is. I saw——'

'And searched before we left.'

'I tell you I saw his foot in the chart locker. Go and look for yourself.'

'You're sure?'

'Dead certain.'

Dale rose from the control desk and held out his hand.

'Give me that pistol. I'll settle with him. Now we know where the extra weight was.'

He was coldly angry. The presence of a stowaway might easily have meant disaster for all of them. No wonder the ship had lagged a little to begin with, and no wonder that the fuel level had shown an unexpected reading. He pulled himself through the trap-door closely followed by the rest. The front of the locker was still fastened. He twisted the latch and flung it wide open.

'Now then. Out of that!' he ordered.

There was no movement. He jabbed the muzzle of his pistol among the papers and felt it encounter something yielding.

'Come out of it!' he repeated.

The protruding toe stirred, sending a bunch of charts floating out into the room and revealing a high boot laced to the knee. The stowaway began to wriggle slowly out of the opening, feet first. The boots were followed by breeches and a jacket of soft leather, and finally, a woe-begone, grimy face. Dale, after one glance at the dis-ordered hair around it, lowered his pistol.

'Oh, my God, it's a woman,' he said in a tone of devas-tating digust.

'Dear me,' said Froud's voice calmly. 'Just like the movies, isn't it? Quaint how these things happen.'

The girl struggled free of the locker and came drifting across the room. But for her weightlessness, she would have collapsed. She put out her hand to grasp a stan-chion, but did not reach it. Her eyes closed, and she floated inertly in mid-air.

'What's more,' Dale added, 'she's the kind that begins by fainting. What, in heaven's name, have we done to deserve this?'

The doctor caught the girl's arm.

'You can't blame her for that. We all fainted—and we had sprung couches. If she's not broken anything, it'll be a wonder.'

Burns slipped a flask from his pocket.

'Give the lass a drop of brandy,' he suggested.

The doctor thrust him off impatiently.

'Get away, man. How the devil do you think you can pour a liquid here? Do use what brains you've got.'

Burns stood back, abashed and regarding the unpour-able brandy with a bewildered expression.

'You'd better take her into the sick-room and look after her, I suppose,' Dale said grudgingly. 'You'd better clean her up, too. I never saw anyone in such a filthy mess. She's probably ruined some of those charts.'

'If I were you,' advised Froud, 'I'd do the cleaning up before the reviving. She'll never forgive you if she wakes up to see herself as she is now. This part of her performance is well below the movie standard—nobody yet ever saw a film star just after she had been thoroughly ill.'

CHAPTER VIII

JOAN

BACK in the living-room there closed down one of those uncomfortable silences sometimes described as 'palpable'. Dale paused beside the control desk and glanced at the instruments there without seeing them, for his mind was at present entirely possessed by a sense of surging indignation. Burns sat down on the side of the table and placidly awaited the outcome. Froud, attempting to drop comfortably upon one of the couches found this casual gesture defeated by lack of weight, and hung for a time in a state of puzzled suspense. Dugan crossed to one of the unshuttered windows and examined the wonders of space with noticeably discreet attention.

It was Froud who ended the mute period.

'Well. Well. Well,' he murmured, reflectively. 'And here was I thinking that I had got the only all male assignment since sex appeal was invented. It just shows you—even a journalist can be wrong sometimes. You know,' he added, 'old Oscar Wilde had his points in spite of what people said about him.'

Dugan turned from the contemplation of stars, looking puzzled.

'What the devil are you talking about?' he inquired.

'Oh, quite harmless. Only that Wilde had a theory about nature imitating art. The typical art of today is the movies—hence the situation. Who but the movie-minded would have thought of stowing away on a rocket? Therefore——'

53

'That's all very well,' Dale told him, 'but this isn't as funny as you seem to think. And the point at present is what are we going to do about it?'

'Do?' echoed Froud, undismayed. 'Why, that's simple enough—heave her outside.'

'Here, I say——' Dugan began.

Froud grinned at him.

'Exactly. But the fact remains that it is the only thing we can do. The alternative—which we shall undoubtedly adopt—is not to do anything: to lump it, in fact.'

'If it had been a man,' Dale said, 'I'd soon have settled him—and it couldn't have been called murder.'

'But as it *isn't* a man——?'

'Well, damn it all, why not? A woman doesn't eat less or breathe less. Is there any really good reason why she shouldn't be treated the same way?'

'None at all,' said Froud promptly. 'Equal pay for equal work, equal penalties for equal crimes, and all that. Entirely logical and correct procedure. But no one ever puts it into practice—this is known as chivalry,' he explained, kindly.

Dale, engrossed with the problem, took no notice.

'She's just trading on her sex, as they all do—that's what it is. Taking it for granted that just because she happens to be a woman we shall do her no harm.'

'No—be fair to her,' the journalist said. 'It's your sex that she's trading on. If the *Gloria Mundi* had had a crew of women, she'd soon have been outside. But she argues that you, being a male, won't behave logically—what's more, she's perfectly right.'

'Can't you be serious for a few minutes?'

'Oh, I am. I'm facing a terrible future which you chaps haven't thought of yet. By the time she's been here a week she'll be bossing the whole show and making us feel as if we were the supercargo instead of she. I know 'em.'

'*If* she stays.'

'Oh, she'll stay all right. I really don't know why you're making all this fuss. You know quite well none of us has guts enough to chuck her overboard, and that we'll just have to accept the situation in the end.'

'That's right,' Dugan put in. 'Anyway, she's done the really serious part of the damage already by coming at all. There'll be enough food to see us through. And I mean to say, we can't just—er—bump her off, can we?'

He turned to Burns who nodded silent support.

Dale looked at the three faces. He wore a somewhat deflated appearance not surprising in one who felt himself to be showing weakness in the face of the trip's first emergency. He took refuge on a side-track.

'Well, I'd like to know who got her aboard. I know none of you would play a damn-fool trick like that, but when we get back, I'm going to find out who did, and, by God——' The return of the doctor cut short his threat.

'Well?'

'Given her a sedative. She's sleeping now.'

'Nothing broken?'

'Don't think so. Pretty well bruised, of course.'

'H'm, that's a blessing, at least. It would have been about the last straw to have been landed with an invalid.'

'I don't think you need bother about that. She'll probably be all right in a day or two.'

'And in the meantime,' said Froud, 'all we can do is to await this probably disruptive influence with patience.'

A full forty-eight hours passed before Doctor Grayson would allow his patient to be seen, and even then his permission was given reluctantly. So far, he told them, she had made a good recovery, but now the thought of her reception was beginning to worry her and retard progress. He considered it worth the risk of a slight setback to have matters out and let the girl know where she stood.

Dale immediately made for the trap-door. It would be easier, he thought, to conduct this first interview in the privacy of the tiny sick-room. To his irritation he found that he did not arrive there alone.

'What do you want?' he demanded, rounding on

Froud.

'Me? Oh, I'm just tagging along,' the other told him placidly.

'Well, you can go back to the rest. I don't need you.'

'But that's where you're wrong. I am, as it were, the official record of this trip—you can't start by censoring me the moment something interesting happens.'

'You'll know all about it later.'

'It wouldn't be the same. Must have the stowaway's first words and the captain's reactions. I'm afraid you've not got the right angle on this, Dale. Now, here is Romance—with a capital R——'

He shook his head at Dale's grunting snort.

'Oh, yes it is—in spite of your noises. It's axiomatic in my profession. The unexpected appearance of any girl is always Romance. And I am the representative of the world population—two thousand million persons, or thereabouts, all avidly clamouring for Romance—is it fair, is it decent, that you for a mere whim should deprive——?'

'Oh, all right. I suppose you'd better come. Only for God's sake don't talk so damn' much. In fact, don't talk at all—if you can manage that without bursting.'

He opened the door, and the two of them crowded into the little place.

The interval had worked a wonderful transformation in the stowaway's appearance. It was difficult to believe that the girl who lay on the slung couch and examined her visitors with calm appraisement could be identical with the figure of misery which had emerged from the locker. Both men were a little taken aback by the serious, unfrightened regard of her dark eyes. Neither had known quite what attitude to expect, but their surmises had not included this appearance of detached calm. Dale returned her look, momentarily at a loss. He saw an oval face, tanned to a soft brown and framed by darkly gleaming curls. The features were small, fine and regular; a firm mouth, with lips only a shade redder than nature had intended, and, below it, a chin suggesting resolution without stubbornness. Insensibly, when faced with the particular cause, he modified his attitude to the situation in general, and from its beginning the interview progressed along lines he had not intended.

'Well?' the girl asked evenly.

Dale pulled himself together. He began as he had meant to begin, but he felt that there was something wrong with the tone.

'I am Dale Curtance, and I should like an explanation of your presence here. First, what is your name?'

'Joan,' she told him.

'And your surname?'

Her gaze did not waver.

'I don't think that matters at present.'

'It matters to me. I want to know who you are, and what you are here for.'

'In that case you will be disappointed that I do not choose to give you my other name. If you were to press me I could give you a false one. You have no means of checking. Shall we say "Smith"?'

'We will not say "Smith",' Dale retorted shortly. 'If you will not tell me your name, perhaps you will be good enough to explain why you joined this expedition unasked and unwanted. I suppose you do not understand that just your presence might easily have wrecked us at the very start.'

'I hoped to help.'

'Help?—You?' His contemptuous tone caused her to flush, but she did not drop her eyes. At that moment Froud, watching her, felt some slight stirring of memory.

'I've met you before, somewhere,' he said suddenly.

Her gaze shifted from Dale's to his own face. He fancied that he caught a faint trace of apprehension, but the impression was slight.

'Indeed?' she said.

'Yes, I caught it just then, when you were angry. I've seen you look like that before. Now, where was it?' He knitted his brows as he stared at her, but the answer evaded him. Out of the thousands of girls he met each year in the course of his work, it was remarkable that he should have recalled her at all—which suggested that they must have met in unusual circumstances, but for the life of him he could not place the occasion.

Dale had prepared appropriate sentiments and was not to be deterred from expressing them.

'I suppose,' he said, 'that you're one of those girls who think that they can get away with anything nowadays. Give a show-girl smile, and everyone is only too glad to have you along—and the newspapers lap it all up when you get back. Well, this time you've got it wrong. I'm not glad to have you along—none of us is—we don't want you——'

'Except me,' put in Froud. 'The S.A. angle will be——'

'You shut up,' snapped Dale. To the girl he went on: 'And I'd like you to know that, thanks to your interference, we shall be lucky if we ever do get back. If you'd been a man, I'd have thrown you out—I ought to even though you're a woman. But let me tell you this, you're not going to be any little heroine or mascot here—when there's work to be done, you'll do it the same as the rest. Help, indeed!'

The girl's eyes flashed, nevertheless, she spoke calmly.

'But I shall be able to help.'

'The only way you're likely to help is to give Froud a better story for his nitwit public—only you've probably at the same time spoilt his chance of ever getting back to tell it.'

'Look here,' the journalist began, indignantly, 'my public is not——'

'Be quiet,' Dale snapped.

All three were quiet. The girl shrugged her shoulders and continued to meet Dale's gaze, unabashed by his mood. The silence lengthened. She appeared unaware that some response from her was the natural next step in the conversation. Dale began to grow restive. He was not entirely unused to young women who kept their eyes fixed on his face, but they usually kept up at the same time a flow of chatter accompanied by frequent smiles. This girl merely waited for him to continue. He became aware that Froud was finding some obscure source of amusement in the situation.

'How did you get on board?' he demanded at last.

'I knew one of your men,' she admitted.

'Which?'

She shook her head silently. Her expression was a reproof.

'You bribed him?'

'Not exactly. I suggested that if he got me here, he would be the only one who knew about it and that the *Excess* or the *Hail* might be generous for exclusive information.'

'Well, I'm damned. So by now everybody knows about it?'

'I expect so.'

Dale looked helplessly at Froud.

'And yet,' said the latter reflectively, 'there are still people who doubt the power of the Press.'

Dale turned back once more to the girl.

'But why? Why? That's what I want to know. You don't look the kind who—I mean if you'd not been as you are, I wouldn't have been so surprised, but——' He finished in the air.

'That's not very lucid,' she said, and for the first time smiled faintly.

'I think he's trying to say that you don't look like a sensationalist—that this is not just a bit of exhibitionism on your part,' Froud tried.

'Oh, no.' She shook her head with the curious result that the outflung curls remained outflung instead of falling back into place. Unconscious of the odd effect, she went on: 'In fact, I should think he has a far more exhibitionistic nature than I have.'

'Oh,' said Dale a little blankly as Froud smiled.

Doctor Grayson came to the door.

'Have you two finished now?' he inquired. 'Can't have you tiring my patient out, you know.'

'Right you are, Doc,' said Froud, rising, 'though I fancy you rather underestimate your patient's powers of recovery.'

'What did she say?' Dugan demanded, as they entered the living-room.

'Precious little except that her name is Joan, and that she considers Dale an exhibitionist—which, of course, he is,' Froud told him. Dugan looked puzzled.

'Didn't you ask her why she had done it—and all that?'

'Of course.'

'Well?'

Froud shrugged his shoulders and pushed the familiar lock of hair back from his forehead.

'This looks like being a more interesting trip than I had expected.' He looked at the other three, thoughtfully. 'Five of us and her, cooped up here for three months. If the proportion of the sexes were reversed, there would be blue murder. Possibly we shall just avoid murder, but you never know.'

CHAPTER IX

IDENTIFICATION

DALE's anger at the finding of the stowaway had been due as much to a dread of the consequences of her presence among them as to the practical results of her additional weight. The girl, Joan, was an unknown quantity thrust among his carefully chosen crew. He saw her as the potential cause of emotional disturbances, irrational cross-currents of feeling, and, not impossibly, of violent quarrels which might make a misery of the voyage. The close confinement for weeks would have been a severe enough test of companionship for the men alone, for though he had chosen men he knew well, it was inevitable that he should know them only under more or less normal conditions. How they were likely to react to the changed circumstances, he could only speculate—and that not too happily.

Ultimately it depended upon the character of the girl. If she were level-headed, they might conceivably get through without serious trouble: if not ... And now, ten days out (in the Earth reckoning), he still could not make up his mind about her. To all of them, as far as he knew, she was still that unknown quantity which had emerged from the locker. She had still given no reason for her presence, and yet, in some way, he was aware from her attitude, and as much of her character as she chose to show, that it had been no light whim nor search for notoriety which had driven her into this foolhardy adventure. But if it was not that, what could it be? What else was strong enough to drive an undeniably attractive girl to such a course? She did not seem to have the sustaining force of a specialized interest such as that which had enabled the doctor to face the trip. Her general education was good and her knowledge of astronomy unusual; her comprehension of physics, too, was above the general standard, but it was not an absorbing passion urging her to overcome almost insuperable difficulties. But there must be a reason of some kind ...

But in spite of her retention of confidence he was admitting that they might have been far more unlucky in their supercargo. As Froud had pointed out, they might as easily have been saddled with a fluffy blonde with cinema ambitions. Joan was at least quietly inconspicuous and ready to perform any task suggested to her. He wondered how long that attitude would last.

She was standing close to one of the windows, looking out into space. Most of her time was spent in this way, though after the first novelty had worn off, she did not seem to study the far-off suns; rather, it was a part of her aloofness from the rest of them; as though the unchanging, starry blackness before her eyes set her mind free to roam in its private imaginings. Of the course of these thoughts no sign appeared; there was no play of expression across the sunburned, serious face, no frown as though she sought a solution of problems, no hint of impatience, only sometimes did it appear that her eyes were deeper and her thoughts more remote than at others. Generally the talk of the rest passed her by, unheard, but infrequently a remark chanced to catch her attention, and she would turn to look at the speaker. Rareuy, one had the impression that secretly and privately she might be smiling.

A question of Froud's brought her round now. He was sitting at the table—sitting by force of habit, since neither sitting nor lying was more restful than standing in the weightless state. He was asking Dale:

'I've meant to ask you before, but it's kept on slipping my mind: why did you choose to try for Mars? I should have thought Venus was the natural target for the first trip. She's nearer. One would use less fuel. It was the place Drivers was aiming at, wasn't it?'

Dale looked up from his book, and nodded.

'Yes, Drivers was trying to reach Venus. As a matter of fact, it was my first idea to go for Venus, but I changed my mind.'

'That's a pity. It's always Mars in the stories. Either we go to Mars or Mars comes to us. What with Wells and Burroughs and a dozen or so of others, I feel that I know the place already. Venus would have been a change.'

Dugan laughed. 'If we find Mars anything like the Burroughs conception, we're in for an exciting time. Why did you give up the Venus idea, Dale?'

'Oh, several reasons. For one thing, we know a bit more about Mars. For all we can tell, Venus under those clouds may be nothing more than a huge ball of water. We do know that Mars is at least dry land, and that we shall have a chance of setting the *Gloria Mundi* up on end for the return journey. If we came down in a sea, it would mean finish. Then again, the pull of gravity is much less on Mars, and this ship is going to take some handling even there. I don't know why Drivers chose Venus—probably he didn't want to wait for Mars' opposition or something of the kind. But you were wrong about it needing less fuel. Actually it would use more.'

'But Venus comes about ten million miles closer,' Froud objected, looking puzzled.

'But she's a much bigger planet than Mars. It would take much more power to get clear of her for the return journey. This falling through space uses no fuel. It's the stopping and starting that count, and obviously the bigger the planet, the greater its pull—that is, the more it costs to get free.'

'I see. You mean that as we are now—clear of the Earth's pull—we could go to Neptune or to Pluto, even, with no more cost of power than to Mars?'

'Sure. In fact, we could go out of this system into the next—if you didn't mind spending a few centuries on the journey.'

'Oh,' said Froud, and relapsed into a thoughtful silence.

'I wonder,' the doctor put in generally, 'why we do these things? It's quite silly really when we could all stay comfortably and safely at home. Is it going to make anyone any happier or better to know that man can cross space if he wishes to? Yet here we are doing it.'

Joan's voice came from the window, surprising them.

'It is going to make us wiser. Don't you remember Cavor saying to Bedford in Wells' *First Men in the Moon,* "Think of the new knowledge!"?'

'Knowledge?' said the doctor. 'Yes, I suppose that is it. For ever and for ever seeking knowledge. And we don't even know why we seek it. It's an instinct, like self-preservation; and about as comprehensible. Why, I wonder, do I keep on living. I know I've got to die sooner or later, yet I take the best care I can that it shall be later instead of finishing the thing off in a reasonable manner. After all, I've done my bit—propagated my species, and yet for some inscrutable reason I want to go on living and learning. Just an instinct. Some kink in the evolutionary process caused this passion for knowledge, and the result is man—an odd little creature, scuttling around and piling up mountains of this curious commodity.'

'And finding that quite a lot of it goes bad on him,' put in Froud. The doctor nodded.

'You're right. It's far from imperishable. I suppose there is some purpose. What do you suppose will happen when one day a man sits back in his chair and says: "Knowledge is complete"? You see, it just sounds silly.

We're so used to collecting it, that we can't imagine a world where it is all collected and finished.'

He looked up, catching Dugan's eye, and smiled.

'You needn't look at me like that, Dugan. I'm not going off my rocker. Have a shot at it yourself. Why do you think we are out here in the middle of nothing?'

Dugan hesitated 'I don't know. I've never really thought about it, but I've a sort of feeling that people grow out of—well, out of their conditions just as they grow out of their clothes. They have to expand.'

Joan's voice surprised them again as she asked Dugan:

'Did you ever read J. J. Astor's *Journey to Other Worlds*?'

'Never heard of him. Why?' Dugan asked.

'Only that he seemed to feel rather the same about it, right back in 1894, too. As far as I remember he said: "Just as Greece became too small for the civilization of the Greeks, so it seems to me that the future glory of the human race lies in the exploration of at least the Solar System." Almost the same idea, you see.'

The doctor looked curiously at the girl.

'And is that your own view, too?'

'My own view? I don't know. I can't say that I have considered the underlying reasons for my being here; my immediate reasons are enough.'

'I'm sorry you won't confide them. I think you would find us interested.'

The girl did not reply. She had turned back to the window and was staring out into the blackness as though she had not heard. The doctor watched her thoughtfully for some moments before returning to the rest. Like Dale he was now quite certain that no mere whim had led her to board the *Gloria Mundi*, and he was equally at a loss to ascribe any satisfactory reason for her presence. His attention was recalled by Froud saying:

'Surely the cause of our being here really lies in our expectations of what we shall find on Mars. The doc is primarily a biologist, and his reason is easy to understand. I, as a journalist, am after news for its own sake.'

'Superficially that is true,' the doctor agreed, 'but I was wondering at the fundamental urge—the source of that curiosity which has sent generation after generation doing things like this without seeming to know why. I suppose we all have our own ideas of what we shall find, but I don't mind betting that not one of those expectations, even if it is fulfilled, is a good enough cause, rationally speaking, for our risking our lives. I know mine isn't. I expect to find new kinds of flora. If I do, I shall be delighted, but—and this is the point—whether it proves useful or quite useless I shall be equally delighted at finding it. Which makes me ask again, why am I willing to risk my life to find it?'

Froud broke in as he paused:

'It is really the same as my reason. News gathering. The difference is that your news is specialized. We are all gatherers of news—which is another name for knowledge—so now we're back where you started.'

'Well, what do you expect to find?' the doctor asked him.

'I don't really know. I think most of all I want evidence of the existence of a race of creatures who built the Martian canals.'

Dugan broke in.

'Canals! Why, everybody knows that that was a misconception from the beginning. Schiaparelli just called them *canali* when he discovered them, and he meant channels. Then the Italian word was translated literally and it was assumed that he meant that they were artificial works. He didn't imply that at all.'

'I know that,' Froud said coldly. 'I learnt it at school as you did. But that doesn't stop me from considering them to be artificial.'

'But think of the work, man. It's impossible. They're hundreds of miles long, and lots of them fifty miles across, and the whole planet's netted with them. It just couldn't be done.'

'I admit that it's stupendous, but I don't admit that it's impossible. In fact, I contend that if the oceans of the

Earth were to dry up and our only way of getting water was to drain it from the poles, we should do that very thing.'

'But think of the labour involved!'

'Self-preservation always involves labour. But if you want to shake my faith in the theory that the Martian canals were intelligently constructed, all you have to do is to account for their formation in some other way. If you've got an idea which will explain nature's method of constructing *straight*, intersecting ditches of constant width and hundreds of miles in length, I'd like to hear it.'

Dugan looked to Dale for assistance, but the latter shook his head.

'I'm keeping an open mind. There's not enough evidence.'

'The straight lines are evidence enough for me,' Froud went on. 'Nature only abhors a vacuum in certain places, but she abhors a straight line anywhere.'

'Aye,' Burns agreed, emerging unexpectedly from his customary silence. 'She can't draw a straight line nor work from a plan. Hit and miss is her way—an' a lot of time she wastes with her misses.'

'Then, like me, you expect to find traces of intelligent life?' the journalist asked him.

'I don't know, that's one of the things I'm hoping to find out. Though now you're asking me, I never did see why we should think that all God's creatures are to be found on one wee planet.'

'I'm with you there,' the doctor agreed. 'Why should they? It seems to me that the appearance of life is a feature common to all planets in a certain stage of decay. I'd go further. I'd say that it seems likely that in one system you will find similar forms of life. That is, that anywhere in the solar system you will find that life has a carbon basis for its molecules, while in other systems protoplasm may be unknown though life exists.'

'That's beyond me,' Dugan told him. 'Are you trying to lead up to a suggestion that there are, or were, men on Mars?'

'Heavens no! All I am suggesting is that if there is life it will probably be not incomprehensibly different in form from that we know. Fundamentally it will depend on the molecules of oxygen, nitrogen, hydrogen and carbon which go to make up protoplasm. What shapes it may have taken, we can only wait and see.'

'What a unique opportunity for reviving the traveller's tale as an institution,' put in Froud. 'We could have a lot of fun telling yarns about dragons, unicorns, cyclops, centaurs, hippogriffs and all the rest of them when we get home.'

'You've forgotten that you're the camera man of this expedition. They'd demand photographs,' Dale reminded him. Froud grinned.

'The camera never lies—but, oh, what a lot you can do with a photograph before you print it. It'll be amusing,' he went on, 'to see which of the story-tellers was nearest the truth. Wells, with his jelly-like creatures, Weinbaum, with his queer birds, Burroughs, with his menageries of curiosities, or Stapledon, with his intelligent clouds? And which of the theorists, too. Lowell, who started the canal irrigation notion, Luyten, who said that the conditions are just, but only just, sufficient for life to exist at all, Shirning, who——?'

He stopped suddenly. The rest, looking at him in surprise, saw that he had turned his head and was looking at the girl. And she was returning his stare steadily. Her expression told them nothing. Her lips were slightly parted. She seemed to breathe a little faster than usual. Neither of them spoke. Dugan said:

'Well, what did what's-his-name say, anyway?'

But the rest took no notice. The doctor was frowning slightly, as if in an effort of memory. Dale looked frankly bewildered, the more so for he noticed that even Burns' attention had been caught. Froud, with his eyes still on the girl's face, raised his eyebrows interrogatively. She hesitated for a second and then gave an all but imperceptible nod.

'Yes,' she said slowly, 'I suppose they'll have to know now.'

Froud twisted round to face the others.

'Gentlemen, the mystery of the *Gloria Mundi* is solved. I present, for the first time on any space ship, Miss Joan Shirning.'

The effect of the announcement was varied.

'So that was it,' the doctor murmured half aloud, as he looked at the girl again. Burns nodded, and eyed her in the manner of one reserving judgment. Dugan goggled, and Dale merely increased his expression of bewilderment.

'What's it all about?' he asked irritably.

'Good Lord, man. Surely you can't have forgotten the Shirning business already?'

'I seem to have heard the name somewhere, but what and when was it?'

'About five years ago. Grand newspaper stunt. Started off great and then flopped dead. You couldn't help——'

'I must have been away, besides, I spent the last part of 1976 in a Chinese hospital over that Gobi Desert crash. What was the Shirning business?'

Froud looked at the girl again.

'Miss Shirning will be able to tell you about it better than I can, it's her story.'

'No.' Joan shook her head. 'I'd rather you told what you know of it first.'

After a moment's hesitation Froud agreed.

'All right. And then you can fill in the details. As far as I can remember, it went like this. John Shirning, F.R.S., D.Sc., etc., was professor of Physics at Worcester University. It's not a large place, and they were lucky to have him, because he was a biggish shot in the physics world. However, he'd been there several years, and it seemed to suit him all right. Well, sometime in the autumn of 1976 he mentioned to a friend, in confidence, that he had come by a remarkable machine which he could not understand either in principle or operation. As far as he knew, it was unique, and in the course of the conversation, he let slip the suggestion that it might even be of extra-terrestrial origin.

'Well, the friend was less of a friend than Shirning

68

thought. Either he really thought that Shirning was going dotty, or else he wanted to create the impression that he was. Anyway, he started spreading the yarn left and right. Now, mind you, if it had been about any Tom, Dick or Harry, nobody would have taken any notice, but because the tale was hitched on to Shirning, people began to get curious. They started hinting about it and soon got to asking him outright what this mysterious thing was, and he made the primary mistake of not denying the whole thing and stamping on it then and there. Instead, he told them to mind their own damned business, which, of course, they did not. Then, after a bit, the Press got hold of it, and started being funny at his expense.

'The University faculty stood it for a week or so, and then they tackled him. Told him he was making the place a laughing-stock, and would he please give a public denial of the story right away. Then he shook them a bit by saying he couldn't do that because, in his opinion, it was the truth. Of course they opened their eyes, pulled long faces, shook their heads and didn't believe him—and you can hardly blame them. So, to cut it short, he said that the thing, whatever it was, had been in his house for nearly a month now and he was more convinced than ever that no one on Earth had the knowledge necessary to make it. And if they didn't believe him, he'd show it to them the next day—what was more, he'd show it to the Press, too, and he defied any of them to explain what the thing was, or on what principles it worked.

'The following day he allowed about twenty-five of us to come to the show—I was covering it for the *Poster*— and we were all crowded into one room of his house while he gave a great harangue about his machine. We listened, some of us bored, and some of us quite impressed, while the University authorities looked just plain worried. Then he said we should see for ourselves. He had just opened the door to lead us to his lab. when his daughter—by the way, I apologize to Miss Shirning for being so long in recognizing her—when she came running in to say that the thing had gone.'

'You mean stolen?' Dale asked.

'No, that would have been fishy enough at the critical moment, but this was worse. She said it had dissolved itself with chemicals in the lab. Shirning sprinted along with the rest of us behind him. All we saw was a large pool of metal all over the floor, and he went nearly frantic . . .

'Well! I mean to say! Can't you imagine the results? It was a gift to the cheap rags. They made whoopee with it, and tore Shirning to bits for a public holiday. He had to resign his post right off. It was the end of him as far as his career was concerned.

'But, if it was a stunt, the most puzzling thing about it was, why should he do it? And, even more pertinently where a man of his talent was concerned, why should he do it so badly? A man of his standing had no need of even mild stunts for self-advertisement, let alone an impossible thing like this. The most charitable talked darkly of overwork, but he didn't look overworked to me. After that, he and Miss Shirning disappeared, and it all petered out as these things do.

'That's a straight view of the public side of the affair, isn't it, Miss Shirning?'

'That's what happened, Mr. Froud. And considering what most of the other journalists there wrote in their papers afterwards, I think you are being very fair.'

'Don't be too hard on them. They had to earn their bread.'

'They earned it by breaking my father.'

'Sounds like nonsense to me,' Dale put in. 'Do you mean to tell me that Shirning actually claimed that this machine was not made on Earth, at all? That it got there from another planet?'

'To be accurate,' the girl told him, 'it came from Mars.'

'Oh,' said Dale, and a prolonged silence fell over the living-room of the *Gloria Mundi*.

'You still stick to it, then, both of you?' Froud said, at last.

'We do.'

'And so I suppose we have found out at last why you are here?'

'Yes.'

'I don't see that that gives you any good reason for stowing away on my ship,' Dale said. 'Even if you do stand by such a fantastic yarn, we should find out what there is on Mars whether you're with us or not.'

'I told you before that I came to help,' said the girl calmly. 'I wrote to you, but you didn't answer my letter, so I came.'

'You wrote! My God! The moment the news of this flight got out half the world started writing to me. I had to have a batch of secretaries to sort the mail. They put the stuff into piles: would-be passengers, mystic warnings, crazy inventors, plain nuts, beggars, miscellaneous. Which was yours? The odds are in the favour of "plain nuts"; it was the biggest class.'

'I offered my services.'

'Of course. So did a million or so others. How?'

'As an interpreter.'

Another withering silence fell on the room. Froud was unable to restrain a chuckle as he caught sight of Dale's face.

'Look here, young woman,' said the latter, when he had recovered his power of speech, 'are you trying to have a game with me? If so, I don't think it's very funny.'

'I'm perfectly serious.'

'Evidently it was the "plain nuts" list. However, I can play, too. May I ask what University is now giving degrees in conversational Martian?'

Joan continued to face him unabashed. She said, slowly:

'Nor is that very funny, Mr. Curtance. I can't speak it, but I *can* write it. I fancy that I am the only person on Earth who can—though I may be wrong in that.'

'No,' said Dale, 'don't qualify. I'm thoroughly prepared to believe that you're unique.'

She studied him for a moment.

'In this matter, I am. And,' she added, 'I have also had a unique opportunity of studying the particular type of facetiousness to which the subject gives rise. I suggest that as you have now allowed your reflexes to relieve themselves in the conventional style, you might, just for the time being, control your brain after the manner of an intelligent person.'

'Atta girl!' murmured Froud appreciatively, during the subsequent pause.

Dale reddened. He opened his mouth to speak, and then thought better of it. Instead, he relapsed into a condition akin to sulks.

'Miss Shirning,' said Froud, 'as you know, I was at that meeting at your father's house. I didn't think it funny, as the others mostly did. I knew your father's reputation too well to put it down as a hoax. Besides, nobody watching him closely could have had any doubt that he believed every word he was saying. But after the anticlimax, of course, he could do nothing, and neither of you would tell us a word more of the story. What was it?'

'What good would it have been? We'd lost the only true proof—the machine itself. Anything we could have said would have been more fuel for the humorists.' She looked at Dale as she spoke.

'Machine!' said the doctor, emerging explosively from his silence. 'You keep on talking about a machine. Good heavens, girl, there are thousands of different kinds of machines, from sewing-machines to mechanical navvies. What was this language-teaching machine of yours—a kind of tele-typewriter?'

'No. Nothing like that. Nothing like anything we know. I can show you, if you're really interested.'

'Of course I'm interested. If it's true, I'm interested in what you found. If it's not true, I'm interested in your mental condition. The one thing I'm sure about was that it wasn't an intentional hoax, or you wouldn't be here. Is that fair enough?'

'All right,' she agreed. She fumbled in a pocket and produced half a dozen pieces of paper. 'After it destroyed itself, our only record was a movie we had made of it. These are enlargements from that film.'

The doctor took the photographs. Froud came behind him and looked over his shoulder. In the background he recognized a view of Shirning's house at Worcester, but the object on the lawn in the foreground caused him to give an exclamation of surprise. It appeared to consist of a metallic casing, roughly coffin-shaped and supported horizontally upon four pairs of jointed metal legs. Four of the pictures were taken from various angles to give a good idea of the whole, and one of them, which included Joan Shirning standing beside it, enabled him to estimate the length of the casing at a few inches under six feet. Another was a close-up of one end, showing a complicated arrangement of lenses and other instruments grouped upon the front panel, and the last gave detail of a section of the side, showing the attachment to the casing of two lengths of something looking not unlike armoured hose save that each piece tapered to its free end. Looking again at the full-length photographs Froud saw that, in some, all four of these side members were closely coiled against the body of the machine, while, in others, they were outstretched, apparently in the act of waving about.

'Dear me,' he said thoughtfully. 'So that was the great Whatsit as it appeared in life.'

The doctor grunted. 'But what did it do? What was it for? People don't just make machines because they like them, they make them to do something.'

'That,' said Joan, 'is exactly what we thought. It could do quite a lot of things. But my father thought—still thinks, in fact—that its primary purpose was communication.'

Dale silently held out his hand, and the doctor passed the photographs across, saying to the girl:

'Won't you tell us the whole thing from the beginning and let's see what we can make of it?'

'I second that,' Froud added.

The girl glanced at the other three. They said nothing. Dale was looking in a puzzled fashion at the photographs. Dugan avoided her eye. Burns maintained his stolid, non-committal front.

Joan made up her mind. 'I will, but on condition that you don't interrupt, and that you keep your questions till the end.'

The two men nodded.

CHAPTER X

JOAN TELLS

On the twenty-third of September, that year (she began), my father had gone over to Malvern on some business which I forget now. It was just after dusk when he started to motor home to Worcester. The distance, as you probably know, is not far, no more than ten miles, and less than that to our house, for we lived on the Malvern side of Worcester. He had covered about one-third of the distance and was slowing down for a corner which is awkward because it coincides with a farm-crossing, when he heard a loud shout of alarm. A man ran out of the farmyard on the right at top speed. My father just managed to miss him by violent braking as he crossed the road. At the same time there was a great clattering of hooves and two heavy cart-horses, snorting with terror, thundered out of the gateway. They swerved at the sight of the car and one missed it entirely, but the other lurched against it, buckling up one wing like cardboard and smashing the side lamp. It staggered a bit, then it recovered itself and galloped off.

My father, not unreasonably, was very annoyed. Not only had his car been damaged, but he considered himself very lucky not to have been involved in a nasty accident through no fault of his own. He had caught a glimpse of the frightened face of the man who had dashed across his lights, and there was no doubt that the horses were terrified. He stopped his engine and listened for a moment to the hoof-beats clattering away down the road before he got out to investigate. The damage was purely superficial and would not affect the car's running, but he determined to make his complaint at the farm before he went on. By this time the daylight was almost gone and it seemed darker to him than it actually was, for he had been using his headlights. That is why he was half-way across the yard before he saw the machine.

It was standing close by a dung-heap on the far side, and once he had seen it, he was surprised that he had not caught sight of it the moment he passed the gate, for against the darkness of the sheds its polished metal gleamed with a brightness altogether unexpected in farm implements. He stopped and stared at it, seeing more details as his eyes grew accustomed to the dusk. He was intrigued because he could not conceive of its purpose, and he approached it more closely out of curiosity.

Oddly enough, he entirely failed to connect it with the alarm of the man and the horses. Probably as his interest was aroused, they temporarily slipped his mind.

Well, I've shown you pictures of the machine. What did you make of it at first sight? My father, finding it in the semi-darkness, and predisposed to consider it some kind of farm implement, could make nothing of it at all. There it stood, a box-like body on eight jointed supports, with its other members curled up, two on each side, looking like large spiral sea-shells, and its lenses glinting a little in what light was left. He walked right round it, growing more and more puzzled, for he could see no projection which looked like a control, no means of starting it to work, and, most mysterious of all, no indication whatever of the kind of work it might do once it were started. It struck him as strange, too, that a brand-new machine should be left in the open like that without even a cover.

He went up to it and put his hand on the casing. The metal was quite cold, but he fancied he felt the slightest tremble of vibration, as though perhaps a smoothly mounted gyroscope were running inside it. He put his ear against it to listen, and there seemed to be a suggestion of a low, faint thrumming. Then he was suddenly startled. One of the metal spirals uncoiled itself and reached out like a feeler. It gave him a shock, he says, not

75

only because it was unexpected, but because it happened in complete silence. He retreated a few paces, thinking he must have touched a control by accident, and wondering what the result would be. Then he learnt what had scared the horses. The thing began to walk towards him . . .

My father is, I think, as brave as most men, but no braver, and he did what most men would have done. He ran.

And the machine followed. He could hear its metal feet scuttering behind him.

He jumped into his car and started it up. With the engine roaring, he slammed in the gear and let in the clutch. But the car did not take up as it should. Something seemed to be holding it back. Suddenly there was a cracking and rending and he shot forward. He looked back, but he could see nothing in the darkness. Glancing over the side of the car, he found that the whole running-board and rear wing had been torn away. He soon got into top, and with the car humming along satisfactorily his panic calmed a little. In fact, he began to feel thoroughly ashamed of himself, the more so when he realized that he, an educated man, had reacted in precisely the same way as the labourer and the horses. He began to tell himself that he couldn't leave the matter like this—that his own self-respect demanded that he should go back and discover what kind of a machine it could be, and that he must have been mistaken in thinking that it was following him. Whether or not he would have gone back, I don't know, for while he was trying to make up his mind, he happened to look to his right and saw that the machine was running alongside.

He clutched at the wheel, the car swerved and bumped on to the grass verge. He managed to get it back, missing a telegraph post by inches, then he stole another glance to his side, hoping to find that he had been mistaken; but there was no hallucination, the machine was still running level with him.

Then he really gave way to panic. He put his foot on the accelerator and let the car full out. The speedometer went up into the seventies, and for some seconds he was fully occupied with keeping on the road. Not until he reached a straight stretch did he have a chance to look round. When he did, it was to find that the machine was making quite as good a pace as himself. Just then a car appeared ahead. The machine gleamed in its headlights and he saw it drop back to give the other room to pass. He made a desperate effort to force a few more miles an hour out of his car, but it was no good, a few seconds after the other car had passed the machine had drawn level again.

He had to slow down for the lanes near home. They were narrow enough to force the machine behind again and for a time he hoped that it had given up. He swung into our drive, braking hard, and before the engine had stopped turning he was out of his seat, running for the front door. He had just got it open when there was a scuttering on the gravel behind him. He turned, but too late; the thing was half across the threshold when he tried to close the door. It just pushed him aside and forced its way in.

And there it stayed. We were both terrified of it at first, and I don't understand now why we didn't run somewhere for help. I suppose we must have been even more afraid of its following us out into the darkness than of staying in the house with it. Indoors we did at least have light to see what it was doing.

And it did nothing. I came downstairs to see my father standing in the hall and looking at it in a helpless way. He told me not to come any closer, and explained what had happened. I was a little incredulous, but he certainly was looking very shaky. I suggested that he should have some brandy, and to my amazement, when we went into the dining-room, the machine followed.

The brandy helped to restore his balance and to get rid of some of his fright. After all, whatever the thing was, it didn't seem to be dangerous. And, seeing it more clearly, his curiosity grew again. Not only was it quite unlike anything he had ever heard of, but some of its principles were quite novel. A machine capable of running at seventy miles an hour on legs was astounding enough, but other things worried him still more, for instance, nobody, to the best of my knowledge, has succeeded in making prehensile metal tentacles such as this machine carried. Then, while he was still staring at it, the most incredible thing of all happened—it spoke. At least, a strange metallic chattering came from one of the diaphragms set close to the front lenses——

(Joan paused and looked at her audience. None of the five made any remark. She went on.)

—The thing had apparently come to stay, and after a while we were in no hurry to lose it. My father quickly became ashamed of his earlier fright and grumbled at his loss of faith in himself. 'No better than a savage,' he would say. 'My first reaction to the incomprehensible was superstitious funk. Just like a savage who sees a motor-car for the first time. I've only a thin crust of reason, through which the barbarism is likely to break at any moment——' And he went on in this strain until he had resurrected his self-respect to the point where the machine was no more frightening than a clockwork mouse. But his interest in it increased almost to an obsession. He became afraid that other people would find out about it and want to remove it before he had discovered its secret. Save in that one incautious moment that Mr. Froud told you about, I don't believe he mentioned it to a soul. He would spend hours a day examining it and trying to find out how it worked, but he never did. One time he even went as far as to remove the upper part of the casing, but he could make nothing of the machinery inside; he could not even comprehend the motive force; it was something utterly and completely new to him. When he became too interested and started poking about inside, it slowly uncoiled one of its tentacles, pushed him gently aside and replaced its cover itself.

As for me, I didn't attempt to understand it. I just accepted it as a puzzle, and though it took me longer than it did him to lose my fear of it, I found myself after a few days thinking of it as—what shall I say?—perhaps as a sort of large dog—a very intelligent large dog——

(Froud, unable to restrain himself, interrupted her for the first time: 'What did your father think it was?')

—He quite soon began to think, as he still thinks, that it was a kind of remote control mechanism operated and powered from its place of origin. It had several of the senses. It could see, it seemed to hear, it certainly had a tactile sense and the noises which came from its diaphragm must have been speech of a kind, though we could make nothing of it. He got it into his head that it had been sent to establish communication between us and its makers, and, in effect, was a kind of transmitting and receiving station made self-portable. He evolved the idea that perhaps the conditions on Earth were unsuitable for the race that had built it, although they had found a way of crossing space, and so they had constructed this ingenious way of getting round the difficulty.

On that theory he started working to develop two-way communication. When we found that the vocal language was hopeless, we began on diagrams and signs. We established to our satisfaction that its place of origin was Mars, but it was less easy to understand what kind of space ship had brought it. Later on, we began to be able to translate slowly and with a lot of difficulty its written language. It left quite a lot of that behind. But just as we were hoping that communication would soon be fluent, it destroyed itself, as you heard.

Joan stopped speaking, and through a period of increasing discomfort each of the men waited for another to speak. She looked from face to face, her own expression quite inscrutable. It was Dale who broke the spell. His tone was coldly contemptuous.

'And so you've no proof of a single word of all this except these?' He pointed to the photographs.

'None,' she told him calmly.

'Well, I've heard a few fairy-tales in my time, but this——' He left the sentence uncompleted. When he went on, it was in a different tone: 'Come on, you're

79

here now and you can't be sent back, why not tell me the truth? Who put you up to this game? Movie company, news-agency, what was it?'

'Nobody "put me up to it". I wanted to come, and I came. Nobody knew anything about it except the man who helped me. I didn't even tell my father—I left a letter for him.'

'Now, look here, I won't take it out on you, but I just want to know who's behind it, that's all.'

'And I tell you there's no one.' For a moment she glared at him. Then, deliberately controlling her rising anger, she went on:

'I'll tell you why I'm here. It's because I intend to clear my father and myself. We were branded as a pair of liars. He was thrown out of his job. We had to change our names and go to live in a place where no one knew us. For the last four years we've been exiled to a miserable village in the Welsh mountains. Scarcely anyone we knew in the old days will speak to us now if we happen to meet them. Either they think we're swindlers, or else they smirk when they fancy we're not looking and tap their heads. When the chance came to *prove* that we were right, do you think I was going to let it slip? I'm going to see for myself that we were right, and I'm going to tell the world about it when we get back.'

'Good girl,' said Froud approvingly.

Dale rounded on him.

'Good God! You don't mean to say that you believe this crazy yarn? Of all the damned thin tales I ever heard—why, I could think up a better one myself in ten minutes.'

'Quite. So could I. So could Miss Shirning. So could anybody. And that's one pretty good reason for believing it.'

Dale grunted with devastating contempt.

'And I suppose that the sight of a badly built house convinces you that the builder's materials are first class?' he said.

'A poor analogy. I know what's getting you down— and so do you, only you won't admit it. It's the thought

80

that if you believe Miss Shirning, you've got to admit that something else has crossed space in the opposite direction, and that your *Gloria Mundi* won't be the first across after all.'

'Indeed? Now, let me tell you something. The reason why you're believing this rubbish is because you've spent so much of your life writing romantic vomit for morons that the mushy bit of brain you did have has gone rancid. You can go to hell. I'm sick of this twaddle.' He crossed the floor and pulled himself through the trap-door, closing it behind him.

Froud looked across at Joan, and grinned.

'One in the eye for me.'

'What will he do?'

'What can he do except cool off after a bit? Now, just to clinch things, what about giving me my first lesson in literary Martian?'

CHAPTER XI

HALF-WAY

THE occupants of the *Gloria Mundi* settled down into a routine. From custom they split up their time into days and hours according to the clock which showed terrestrial reckoning, and by it they arranged the frequency of meals and sleeping periods. To be able to speak of 'this morning' and 'this afternoon' eased the sense of exile from all familiar things and gave to them all a sense of reality and progress. The view through the surrounding blackness of far-off suns and eternal, unchanging constellations grew depressing when its first novelty had worn off. It became impossible to believe that they were still dropping through space at the rate of seven miles a second; they felt, rather, that everything outside the rocket was wrapped in a state of suspended animation, and that conscious existence was only to be found in themselves and in the clock which ruled the living-room.

But in spite of precautions boredom was not easily

fended off. They began to think of it as a malignant force waiting to pounce on them in any unfilled moment, bringing with it dissatisfaction, regrets and an insidious suggestion of their futility in attempting the fantastic journey. Boredom had become public enemy number one, for the first week had taught them that once it was allowed to establish itself, it contrived speedily to infect the rest and to cause distressingly anti-social eruptions.

Joan contributed an alleviation when she consented to teach Froud the characters which she claimed to be Martian script. Before long, the doctor was also showing an interest in it. Dugan, too, after a period of non-committal spectatorship, admitted that learning it would help to pass the time, and attached himself to the class. The fact that Froud and the doctor frequently fell into arguments most hindering to progress was, in the circumstances, no disadvantage. Joan had more than enough time to teach them the little she knew, and on such occasions she and Dugan listened, only dropping in occasional words to spur the disputants.

As they grew to know the girl better, Dale's anxiety became less acute. Though he was still without a proper comprehension of the force which had driven her to stow away, he appreciated that she was not the type he had feared. Perhaps it was only Froud who realized that his worry had not been so much ill-founded as ill-directed.

Joan's own perception of the situation was sharper than Dale's, though less comprehensive than Froud's. But her mind was set on a single mark, and objects aside of the direct line lacked something of definition and proportion. In spite of herself she minimized her circumstances in view of her aim—the vindication of her father and herself. Nothing was to be allowed to interfere with that. For the duration of the journey she was putting all other personal considerations aside, intending to become, as far as lay in her power, only an instrument for justice; she imagined that it was possible for her to forget and to make the rest forget for three months that she was a woman.

The part she had cast herself for was that of a young man and an equal, and she did her best to play it. But her intention to treat all the five men with complete impartiality was defeated by Dale and the engineer. Dale remained unfriendly and sometimes aggressive, while Burns was unresponsive, occasionally varying his attitude of indifference with a touch of belittlement. It was impossible for her to treat either of them as she treated the three who took her, or appeared to take her, at the valuation she wished, for both the doctor and Dugan, while still non-committal, had had the grace to regard her story as a hypothesis to be proved or dis-proved later. Burns, on the other hand, continued to dismiss it with silent contempt, and Dale not infre-quently created opportunities for expressing his opinions of it.

It irritated him considerably that they left Joan quite unshaken. She continued to speak of it as a fact, admit-tedly unusual, but not fantastic. All his sharpest barbs shivered exasperatingly on a wall of cool indifference, and she did not show the weakness of attempting retali-ation.

Froud and Grayson had contrived new material for argument. In the course of the lesson they had drifted into a discussion of the comparative merits of ideographic and alphabetical writing. The argument had risen over an attempt to classify the Martian script, but it soon reached the stage where Froud found himself passion-ately asserting the superiority of the ideograph (of which he knew extremely little) while the doctor defended the alphabet.

'Take China,' Froud was saying, with a generous wave of the hand, 'a country with hundreds of dialects. Now, with an alphabet, any man wishing to write for the whole country would have to be translated or else have to learn all those dialects and languages, whereas, with ideographs, what happens——?'

'He has to learn thousands of ideographs,' said the doctor brightly.

'—It means that educated people throughout the country can communicate whatever their language. Now if Europe, instead of having two or three alphabets, wrote purely in ideas, think of the misunderstandings which would have been avoided, and think of the possibilities for international exchange.'

'I don't remember hearing that there was much less misunderstanding in Europe when every educated person spoke and wrote Latin,' the doctor observed. 'And it seems to me that ideographs are not only more limited than words, but even more capable of misinterpretation. Furthermore, is China in its present bogged condition an advertisement for anything? Now, when the Chinese adopt an alphabet——'

'They will also have to invent a kind of Chinese Esperanto. Unless they do, every book will have to be translated into dozens of languages and——'

'Hi,' interrupted Dale. 'Just leave China for a bit and consider where we are.'

'Well,' said Froud, 'where are we?'

'I'll tell you. We're exactly half-way there.'

For some reason they all rose and made for the unshuttered windows and stood there, looking out into the familiar darkness.

'Seems much the same to me,' Froud muttered at last. 'I remember feeling similarly swindled when I crossed the Line for the first time—But then we did have some celebrations,' he added pointedly.

Dale, with the air of a juggler. produced a bottle of whisky from behind his back. He held it up and patted it.

'Brought specially for the occasion,' he told them.

They watched him uncork it. The behaviour of liquids in the weightless *Gloria Mundi* never ceased to fascinate them, and this was an occasion of particular fascination.

Dale held the opened bottle horizontally, pointing towards Joan, and tapped the bottom lightly. A small quantity of whisky drifted out, wobbled a moment, then formed itself into a little amber sphere which wafted slowly across the room. Joan stopped it gently with one finger, leaving it suspended before her.

'Doc,' said Dale, tapping the bottle again.

In a few minutes all six had the translucent golden balls floating in front of them. Dale let go of the bottle and it drifted away.

'Here's to our continued success,' he said.

They put their lips to the liquid and sucked it into their mouths.

'Ah!' said Froud. 'The first in six weeks. I've never been dry so long before. And since one of the advantages of drinking here is that there is no washing up, what about another?'

Joan made her way to the intended sick-room which had become her special cabin. The little celebration had reminded her uncomfortably of her status as an intruder, and the sense that though she was in, she was not of the group, prompted her to leave them to unhampered self-congratulations. She had taken one drink with them, knowing that had she refused, Froud and the doctor at least would have insisted. After that she felt at liberty. She pulled herself on to the couch, fastening the covering partway up so that it might give a comforting sense of weight, and lay listening to the sound of muffled voices.

Back in the living-room, the bottle made its third and last round. Dale had become unwontedly talkative and Froud was watching with a quiet amusement the enthusiastic back-slapping in progress between him, the doctor and Dugan. It appeared that not even the treat of whisky could stir Burns into geniality, for he sat aloof and withdrawn into speculation as if the rest did not exist. Suddenly he hiccoughed twice, made his way to the trap-door and closed it behind him. Dugan laughed.

'See that? A Scot, too. I thought they weaned them on the stuff.'

'Well, we're all a bit out of practice,' said Froud, his eye resting thoughtfully on the closed trap. 'In fact, I'm not at all sure that I have the stomach for neat whisky that I used to have. Honestly, I feel a bit——' He gave a sheepish grin. 'It might be safer if——' He allowed the sentence to trail unfinished as he, too, moved towards the storeroom.

Dugan laughed again.

'And a journalist, too. Don't say you're going to come over queer next, Dale."

Dale shook his head.

'Probably the weightlessness,' suggested the doctor. 'Must be a lot of secondary effects from that, though I must say I feel quite all right myself.'

Froud's grin vanished as he shut the trap-door behind him. He looked round the storeroom and saw no sign of Burns. Stepping as quietly as his metal soles would allow, he made his way to the little sick-room and flung open the door. The place seemed pretty full already, but he managed to slide in.

'Hullo! How interesting,' he remarked.

Burns, handicapped by his lack of weight, had encountered difficulties. In the circumstances, the enterprise of holding down a muscular young woman, even though her movements were hindered by a couch cover, presented unusual problems in mechanics. Moreover, the one hand occupied in covering her mouth was encountering very sharp teeth.

At the sound of the voice Burns turned his head, glowering and breathing heavily.

'Get out, you!'

Froud shook his head.

'The hostess's decision is final.'

'Get out,' Burns said again. But Froud made no move.

'All right, if you won't.'

The engineer shot out a large fist with all his strength behind it. Froud jerked his head aside and the knuckles crashed into the metal door frame. Before the other could move he had driven two rapid short-arm jabs to the stomach. Burns folded up with an agonized grunt.

'Short and neat,' Froud murmured. 'Excuse me.'

He lifted the magnetized shoes out of contact with the floor and towed the man into the storeroom. There he opened the trap-door and thrust him through.

'Hi, Doc,' he called as the engineer's still-gasping form floated into the living-room. 'Job for you. Something seems to have disagreed with him.' He shut the trap and returned to Joan. She still lay on the couch, and she looked up at him as he came in.

'Thank you very much,' she said.

'Not at all,' he assured her. 'Rescue from worse than death is my speciality. I've risked lots of unpopularity that way. There was a girl in San Francisco—it turned out afterwards that he was her husband. You'd never have thought it—most unfortunate.' He paused. 'Any damage?'

'The buttons are off my shirt, otherwise I think he came off worst. And I hope his hand hurts—it tasted nasty.'

'M'm, wouldn't fancy it myself. These engineers, you know. The ingrained oil of years and all that.'

'How did you know about him?' she asked curiously.

'Oh, there was a sultry, broody sort of look in his eye. I've been expecting it. In fact, I expected it before.'

'You were right,' she said, 'only that time it was in the storeroom, and I wasn't at such a disadvantage. I managed to dodge back into the living-room.' She looked at him thoughtfully. 'Anything else?'

'Well,' said Froud non-committally, 'now you come to mention it, there has been an odd-looking scratch on Dale's face for the last four days. He mentioned something about having had a bad shave, and he didn't take it kindly when I asked him if he usually used a circular saw for the purpose.'

Joan nodded. 'He seemed very annoyed about it at the time.'

They looked at one another. Froud admired her attitude to the thing, but had the sense not to put it into words.

'Awkward,' he suggested.

'A nuisance,' she agreed, and added: 'I did wonder if I told Dale I was Burns' mistress, and told Burns I was Dale's, whether that wouldn't head them off?'

Froud shook his head emphatically.

'No, that wouldn't do. It might work with Dale. But Burns is the sort of chap who would merely take it to mean that you weren't very particular. Anyway, there would be an atmosphere of drawn daggers, and they'd probably find out that you'd been spoofing both of them. I knew when I first saw you that this trip was going to be interesting,' he added.

'Stop it! You make me feel like a guinea-pig. I'm prepared to forget for twelve weeks that I'm a woman; why can't they do the same?'

'Perhaps you're not as successful at it as you think you are. Besides, both of them resented your presence here from the start, so up pop our old friends sex-antagonism, desire for domination and the rest of the famous cast. As long as you hold them off, they'll harry you—at least, Burns will—and if you don't hold them off, they'll despise you.'

'Wonderfully cheering, aren't you?' she said.

'Of course, I might take to sleeping in the storeroom,' he suggested.

'Thereby introducing another old friend—propinquity? No, that won't do.'

'I was afraid it mightn't. You know,' he went on, with an air of detachment, 'you're trying the impossible. How, with your figure and your face, you can solemnly expect five normal men for twelve solid weeks to—oh, all right.' He dried up at the sight of her warning expression.

Twenty minutes or so later Froud re-entered the living-room. Burns greeted him with a scowl. Dugan inquired sympathetically if he were feeling better and received an assurance that the crisis had now passed. Froud crossed to the locker devoted to his private belongings and fumbled about in it. Presently he found what he wanted; a small, plated pistol. He took it out and slipped it into his pocket. The others stared in astonishment.

'For Joan,' he explained airily. 'She thought she saw a rat.'

'A rat here? Don't talk rot,' said Dale.

'Oh, I don't know—wonderfully enterprising things,

rats. Anyway, she thought so. Apparently she's a dead shot on rats. She and her father used to pot them in their Welsh cottage by the hundred. So I said I'd lend her this in case she should see it again.'

He left the incredulous group, and returned to the girl.

'Here you are,' he said, handing the weapon across.

She took it, cautiously.

'How do they work? I've never used one before.'

CHAPTER XII

SPECULATION

THE crossing of the invisible half-way mark produced a sense of accomplishment which temporarily, at least, led to a better feeling on board the *Gloria Mundi*. The petty irritation with the personal habits of other people which close proximity aggravates, loomed for the time being less offensively large. The fact that Dale habitually scrubbed his teeth for no less than ten minutes, ceased to count against him; the doctor no longer caused general frowns when he blew his nose with sonorous trumpeting; they ceased to round on Dugan for the unmusical series of yawns with which he announced his wakenings; even Froud was forgiven his irritating habit of drumming with his fingers or indulging in some other irksome mannerism. In the general thaw Dale regained his usual geniality. He appeared to have forgiven Joan's intrusion, seeming to be relieved that she had refused his advances, and more sure of his ground, as a result of the rebuff. At moments Froud even wondered if Dale had been deliberately putting her to the test, but he found himself unable to make up his mind on the point. Whatever the cause, they were thankful for the change and to find that though he still denied the possibility of a Martian origin for Dr. Shirning's machine, yet he was interested in it to the point of questioning Joan for all the details she could give. Though his present attitude was an immense improvement on the contemptuous silence he had maintained, they had not yet prevailed upon him to join the language class.

The exception to this refraternization movement was Burns. He remained a determined and sulky isolationist, seldom speaking to the rest, joining in none of the occupations they devised to pass the time, and watching them out of his aloofness in a way which got on the nerves of the whole party. Indeed, the doctor held that much of the group's newly found mutual tolerance was due to this external source of irritation. Moreover, after regarding the engineer with professional detachment, he became aware of an unprofessional sense of apprehension. Six weeks of the outward journey still to go—and after that, the return trip to be faced ... He decided that he was not happy at the prospect. Burns was, or soon would be, in a state which called for handling with care, and in the circumstances he was scarcely likely to get it.

The thought turned him to a study of the rest. Dale had given him some uneasy moments in the earlier stages, but the reasons had been complicated—responsibility, organization, resentment of the stowaway, troubles before the start, and he understood, too, that Mrs. Curtance had been no help to her husband—in the circumstances, it was understandable that his reactions should be extreme. He was thankful that Dale had got over it so well, and he had little fear now of it reviving.

And Dugan. Well, Dugan had obviously fallen for the girl. That was all to the good—if the girl could maintain her present attitude. The boy was curiously young for his age in some ways—sheep's eyes, and all that, apparently quite content to worship without wanting. Froud? Mentally he shook his head and gave Froud up. Anyway, he imagined that Froud's emotions seldom got the better of his reason. Himself he saw in a kindly avuncular role towards the whole party, the girl included. It would have hurt him considerably to know that Dugan privately regarded him as an unreliable individual of the genus roué.

It was three terrestrial days past the half-way that Joan sprang another surprise on the party.

Dale and Dugan had just finished making one of their periodical checks.

'Dead on the course,' Dale told them. 'It's surprising how little correction we've needed. We know so little of space yet that I was prepared to find all sorts of unguessed sources of deflection.'

'Even so,' Froud put in, 'this three-dimensional navigation business seems pretty tedious. It needs so many readings. Why, if there were much correction to be done, you two would be taking angles and levels and things all the blessed time. I suppose in the days to come, when large passenger liners and freighters go flinging themselves about all over the solar system—and people look back at us and wonder how our little cockleshell survived even the take-off—I suppose then they will all travel on some kind of directional beam system. Like the things they use for air-liners in fogs at home—only, of course, it won't be ordinary radio. The trouble is to find some kind of radiation besides light which will get through the heaviside layers.'

'On the contrary, the trouble is to avoid the cranks who say they've found it already,' Dale told him. 'Why, half the number of experimental transmitters offered to me for this trip would have weighed as much as the *Gloria Mundi* herself.'

'All dud?'

'Most of them certainly. There were one or two I'd like to try sometime, though, but I couldn't afford risking the extra weight this time.'

'You won't need to. Not if we find the creatures which sent Joan's machine. They appear to have solved the problem completely,' Dugan said.

'Provided that control of the machine was exercised from Mars, they do,' the doctor agreed. 'But we've no proof that it was. We mustn't lose sight of the fact that it *may* have been built on Earth.'

'Unlikely,' Froud thought. 'After all, it stands to reason that a man who could invent such a thing is not going to use it just for a joke. Why that dodge of pre-hensile tentacles alone would revolutionize the entire carrying trade.'

The doctor spoke impatiently. 'Of course it's unlikely. The whole thing's unlikely. But there are plenty of pos-sibilities. Even if the machine did come from Mars, there must have been some kind of ship which landed it. Why shouldn't the source of the remote control have been in that ship, and the means used, ordinary radio?'

'But it wasn't ordinary radio,' Joan put in. 'My father looked for that very thing, and there was no sign of it.'

'Well, it seems to me that it must have been controlled from some place on the Earth's surface because the re-sponses were immediate, instantaneous from what you told us—and how do you account for that if the messages had to go all the way to Mars and back?'

'I hadn't thought of that,' Froud admitted.

'I've been wondering,' said Joan, 'when somebody was going to see that difficulty.'

They all looked at her.

'What do you mean?' asked Dugan.

'Well, even light going at 186 thousand miles a second is going to take an appreciable time getting to Mars and back, and there would be an added delay of the opera-tor's responses. And yet the machine's reactions were immediate—faster than ours. I tested that.'

'And according to Einstein, nothing can travel faster than light—so what?' asked the doctor cheerfully.

'That hadn't occurred to me,' Dale admitted. 'Ab-surd, because it's obvious enough once you've men-tioned it. Anyhow, that seems to kill the idea of remote control from Mars.'

'That's what I thought,' said Joan.

They stared at her again.

'Wait a minute. What do you mean—that's just what you thought? Dash it all, you said——' Froud objected.

'Oh no, I didn't. I said that that was my father's theory, and you took it for granted that I believed it, too.'

'But I distinctly remember—at least, I thought I remembered—— Oh well, if that wasn't your idea, what was?'

A little of Joan's assurance left her; she glanced at the faces round her and hesitated; when she spoke, it was with a slightly defiant note.

'It seemed to me to be an individual: a machine that could think for itself.'

The men looked at one another.

'No, hang it all, there are limits,' Froud said, at last.

'I couldn't explain it any other way—can you?'

'What about my idea of control by the ship which brought it?' put in the doctor. But Joan shook her head.

'I tell you, its responses were quicker than our own.'

Froud said: 'You're fooling. You can't really mean it. Why it's—it's preposterous.'

'I know,' she admitted quietly. 'But preposterous or not, there it is. There is only one other possibility and that's my father's explanation—and if he's right, Einstein was wrong. And though I admire my father, my devotion has its limits.

'I was sure almost from the first that it was an—an entity: not just an enlarged tool as other machines are. That's why it frightened me at the beginning, and that's why I never quite lost my fright of it. I suppose it was due to not knowing what it could do, and what its limitations were. You see, it was so—so utterly alien. Yet I thought all the thoughts you are thinking now when I wasn't actually with it. Of course it is ridiculous: such a thing could not possibly be. I used to lie awake at night devising tests for it to prove to myself that it wasn't true. But they didn't prove it. Everything I did seemed to show me more and more clearly that it was an individual, as much cut off from Mars as we were.

'I tell you, when I tested it, it *understood* what I was doing. It used to watch us with its lenses as if it *knew* what was puzzling us. It could look after itself, too; while it was with us, it even replaced one of its damaged feet with a new one which it made itself. I'm prepared to admit that it might have been made to do all that by remote control, except for one thing—the lack of time lag.'

'You mean,' said Dugan, as if the idea had just filtered past his resistance. 'You mean that this thing was a what shall we call it?—a robot?'

'We shall not call it a robot,' said Doctor Grayson. ' "Robot" was a word which Capek used to mean a synthetic human workman, but since Froud's miserable profession took the word up, it's ceased to mean anything. Anyway, there's no synthetic man appearance about this thing.' He turned to Joan. 'The trouble about you is that you're such a level-headed young woman. If almost anyone else I know had come out with a suggestion like that, I'd have recommended a nice long sleep, with a sedative. As it is——' He shrugged.

'It takes some getting used to,' she admitted.

Froud nodded. 'More than that. By the way, this isn't your idea of doing a journalist a good turn and providing him with copy, is it?'

'And yet,' Joan went on, 'when you get used to the idea, it doesn't seem quite so unreasonable, somehow. Machinery must be gradually evolving in some way: why not towards this?' She looked at Dale. 'Have you ever really considered the machine?'

Dale turned a good-humoured, but rather puzzled face. Evidently he meant to let bygones be bygones, for he did not treat her latest fantastic suggestion with the contempt he had poured upon the first. His manner was akin to that of one who conscientiously plays a game within the bounds of rules made by the other player, and he managed with a good grace:

'I don't quite see what you mean—I'm always considering machines. Have been since I was so high, but certainly not the kind that——'

Joan shook her head. 'No, I put it badly. I don't mean the machine we were talking about, nor any particular machine. I was thinking of *The Machine*, considered as a force in the world.'

'In fact, the genus machina,' suggested the doctor.

'Exactly.' Joan nodded emphatically, and then

smoothed back the hair which had become suspended in front of her face. Dale's expression cleared.

'Oh, I see. But it's rather a large and difficult question to answer offhand. I don't seem to see it like that. Being used to them and always among them, I tend to think of machines or machinery, but hardly ever of The Machine. You see, ever since I was little I've been happiest when I was with machinery; it's been a great part of my life. I've known the feel of so many machines, and they've all been different. I can't get outside, as it were, and see the whole range of machines as one class. But I know what you mean, up to a point, because my wife not only can, but frequently does, see The Machine like that. It's one of the points where we've never had anything in common.

'You see, I couldn't do without machines—I don't just mean that I should starve if all machines were broken, that's obvious: about eighty per cent. of the world would starve, too. I mean that they seem to be essential to something in me. A pianist losing his fingers would lose no more than I should if I were entirely deprived of them. They are a great part—to me, the essential part— of the world I grew up in.

'There is use and abuse of machinery as there is of everything else, but when you talk of The Machine, you are seeing it from an angle that I don't know. I think that my wife would understand you better than I do. She quite certainly thinks of The Machine almost as a personification, and she hates it and fears it. Or rather, she hates it because she fears it, and she fears it because she doesn't understand it. The completely primitive attitude—savages are afraid of thunderstorms for the same reason. But she goes further, she is determined not to understand it: even while she lives by it, she tries to pretend to herself that the need for it does not exist and that mankind would be altogether happier and better without machinery. Two minutes' honest thought would reduce the whole attitude to an absurdity in her own eyes, but it seems to be a subject on which she is incapable of a second's honest thought—again, to me, a curiously primitive trait in an otherwise highly civilized person. When one examines her attitude dispassionately, one finds that it has a great deal in common with that of a native who will not examine the nature of his most inimical gods for fear of bringing their wrath down on his head. He ignores them as much as possible to avoid rousing his own fear of them. There must have been something of the kind in Mary Shelley's mind when she conceived that Frankenstein story. I am sure that The Machine is a kind of Frankenstein's Monster in my wife's mind. It is as though the superstition which has been scraped off natural phenomena had attached itself to machinery instead, as far as she is concerned.' He paused as though a new thought had just struck him. 'Yes, that's what it is. Her attitude to machines is rankly superstitious. It sounds rather ridiculous to you, I suppose. But if you could hear her talk about them, I think you'd understand what I mean.'

'I understand you perfectly,' the doctor assured him. 'One's met it so often in women of quite different types —and in a few men, too, of course, but comparatively rarely. If it only occurred in the backward types (where it is almost inevitable), it would be easier to understand. I mean the unintelligent, stupid woman of the domestic class who is afraid of a vacuum-cleaner or of a telephone doesn't surprise one, but the intelligent woman who uses these things and other small machines regularly will frequently *refuse* to understand how they or her car or her gyrocurt work, and will maintain at the back of her mind the same attitude as the stupid woman. It is this *refusal* to learn which is so puzzling. It is possible that a small, almost negligible class may do it with the deliberate idea of encouraging male pride by their own apparent helplessness, and in a few it may be due to sheer mental laziness—but why should so many otherwise mentally active women choose to be lazy on this particular subject? Somewhere and somehow connected with the idea of machinery there arises this curious inhibition.'

'Perhaps it is because women, on the whole, do not

come into contact with machinery as much as men do?' Dugan suggested.

'Again, that might account for a very small number, but nowadays both girls and boys encounter small domestic machines from their earliest consciousness, yet the difference soon begins to show. I'm generalizing, so don't go throwing particular instances of brilliant women engineers at me—in general, I say, the boy becomes intrigued by the intimate details of the machine, but the girl's interest falls behind his: she accepts the fact that the thing works without caring why, and finally she reaches the state when she does not want to know why. She becomes not only uninterested, but antagonistic—and this though her life may at any time depend upon its proper working. Odd, you must admit.'

'Jealousy,' Froud murmured, addressing no one in particular; 'green-eyed monster, et cetera.'

'I thought you'd been silent for a long time. What exactly do you mean by "jealousy" in that cryptic tone?' the doctor asked.

'The highest duty of woman is motherhood,' Froud said. 'It is the crown of her existence. No woman can say she is fulfilled until she has created life with her own life, until she has felt within her the stir of a new life beginning, until she has performed that holy function which Mother Nature has made her glorious task, her mystic joy, her supreme achievement down the echoing ages——'

'What on earth is all this about?' asked the doctor patiently.

Froud raised his eyebrows.

'Don't you like it? My readers love it. It seems to console them a bit for all the actual messiness of reproduction, somehow—makes them forget that cats, rats and periwinkles do the same thing so much more efficiently and easily.'

'Well, just forget your readers for a bit, if you've got anything to say. Try ordinary prose.'

'My art is spurned. All right, at your request, I strip off the rococo. Listen. No one can deny that woman's

97

greatest urge (like you, Doc, I generalize) is creative. If he did try to deny it he would come up against the fact of the race's survival, the life force, George Bernard Shaw and other phenomena. So let us admit that she embodies this intense creative urge.

'So far, so good. But Nature, that well-known postulate, has taken great care that for all its power, its direction shall be severely limited. In other words she has said to herself—"Let woman be creative, but let her create the right things—she mustn't go footling about creating omnibuses, tin-openers or insurance companies—let her creative instinct be concentrated on producing children and on the matters connected therewith."

'I, personally, think it was a mean trick. It has resulted in vast quantities of women in a vastly interesting world being shut into vastly uninteresting compartments. Because, you see, Nature's little scheme necessitated a curtailment of the imagination to keep them on the job. Hence the average woman; history means nothing to her; the future means less (although her children will have to live in that future); world catastrophes are far less interesting than local mishaps. Nature has given her an ingrowing imagination, working chiefly in a bedroom setting. So monotonous.'

'Very quaint,' agreed the doctor, 'but what's all this got to do with——?'

'Ah! I'm just coming to that. The point is this: they simply have not got the imagination to see the machines as we see them, but they have the power to be jealous of them. Women are creators: The Machine is a creator: in that they are rivals. They are afraid of it, too. What is it they fear subconsciously? Is it that man may one day use The Machine to create life?—to usurp their prerogative? They do not know why they fear it, but they resent it. They resent having to share their men with it—they're sulkily jealous. They try to minimize it as though they were dismissing a rival's charms. There is nothing good they can say for it. It's noisy, it's dirty, it's ugly, it's oily, it stinks: and, anyway, it is only a jumble of metal bits—what can be really interesting in that? It is not human and sentient. There you have the crux: the new inhuman creator confronts the human creator.'

'I suppose all that means something,' Dugan said reflectively as Froud stopped.

'Certainly,' agreed the doctor; 'it means that men are more interested in machines than women are.'

'But hadn't you already said——?'

'I had.'

Froud waved a casual hand. 'Oh, go ahead, don't mind me. I merely tried to shed a little light on the troubled waters.'

'Oil,' said the doctor. He turned to Joan.

'Speaking as a woman, what did you think of that mouthful?' he asked.

She smiled. 'Not much.'

'That was only to be expected,' Froud said. 'Now if it were possible for her to speak as a neuter——'

'All the same,' Joan went on, 'most of the women I know who dislike machines dislike them actively. I mean that they dislike them differently from the way in which they dislike, say, an inconvenient house. But then, I should say that such women have resented men's toys all through the centuries, just as men have resented the same type of woman's absorption in domesticity.

'But we seem to have got off the subject. Dale was telling us what he felt about machines, he only instanced Mrs. Curtance to show us what he didn't think, but we haven't let him finish.'

'I don't know that I can, very well. It is, as you say, a feeling. When I think about it, it's difficult to find the words. But I can tell you something of what I don't feel. I don't feel that a good machine is an utterly impersonal thing—a jumble of metal bits, as Froud was saying just now—any more than I feel that a musical composition is a jumble of notes. And it can't be impersonal. Something of the ingenuity, skill and pride of work that went into the making of it remains in it—just as something of the sculptor remains in carved stone.

'And there is a delight in machines, a kind of sensuous delight that derives from smooth running, swiftly spinning bars and wheels, sliding rods, precise swings and the perfect interaction of parts. And, behind it all, a sense of power. Power which, coupled to men's brains, knows no bounds.'

'Power to do what?' Joan asked.

'To do anything—to do everything—perhaps not to do anything. I don't know. Sometimes it seems as if power is the goal in itself: as if a force drove one to master force.'

His words were followed by a silence during which Dugan looked as if he supposed all that also meant something. Joan, noticing his frown, wondered if he disagreed. He shook his head.

'I don't know. You people all make it sound so frightfully complicated. I mean, I like machines all right, they're grand fun to play about with, but I'm hanged if I can see half of what you're talking about. They've just been made for us to use: and a mighty dull world it would be without them. I'd hate to have been born a couple of centuries ago—or even one century ago. Think of not being able to fly! It'd have been—well, I mean to say, what did they do then? Honestly, I don't see what you're getting at. We've got machines; we couldn't get on without them. Naturally, we use them. I don't see what more there is to be said.'

An unexpected voice chimed in for his support. Burns for once was paying some attention to the rest.

'Aye, you're right, lad. Use your machines and use them decently. Don't overdrive them and break their hearts. Look after them an' they'll not let you down—which is more than you can say for some human beings.'

CHAPTER XIII

ARRIVAL

THIS is not the place to lecture upon the details of the inter-planetary journey. If you want the figures of the quantity of explosives used, of the changes consequent upon extra load, rates of acceleration and deceleration, necessary corrections of course, divergencies between theory and performance, etc., you will find them, together with a host of other details, carefully considered in Dale's book, *The Bridging of Space*, and some of them, more popularly arranged, in Froud's *Flight of the 'Gloria Mundi'*. Here, one is interested chiefly in the aspect which neither of these gentlemen saw fit, for one reason or another, to include in his book. And though I believe that Froud toyed for a time with the idea of a less impersonal story of the flight, it is unlikely now that it will ever be written. Almost twelve years have passed since the Mount Wilson observatory lost sight of the *Gloria II*. Whether Dale, Froud and the rest of their party ever reached Venus in her we cannot tell—but she has never returned.

Therefore, if I do not tell you this story as I had it, partly from Joan and partly from the rest, it is likely that it may never be told. But in case you should say to yourself—'these people seem to have talked a great deal, but one feels that they might have done that anywhere. They seem singularly unmoved by the fact that they are taking part in one of history's greatest adventures': in case you say that, let me point out that though travelling through space may be an exciting adventure in prospect and in retrospect, yet in actual accomplishment, I am assured, it is extremely tedious.

It was Dr. Grayson, I think, who said:

'Fancy buying undying fame merely at the cost of six months' close confinement.'

While Froud quoted the classic words of an earlier intrepid flier:

' "It was a lousy trip—and that's praising it." '

But looking back on the journey they get it in perspective and agree that it was not a monotonous whole. The longer view reveals that it fell into distinct phases, each with its own particular complexion. One of the most marked of these was the period which followed Joan's announcement of her belief in a sentient machine.

Whether she timed it by skill or luck, there is no

doubt that the moment was well chosen. Four weeks before, with the memories of everyday life clinging more closely, it would have met with immediate ridicule. But now, from a mixture of motives, it was not airily dismissed. For one thing, they knew the girl better and their attitudes towards her had changed, and, for another, one could not afford, with the threat of a deadly boredom overhanging, to dismiss any subject which showed possibilities of interesting discussion. Her fantastically improbable suggestion had, therefore, a more kindly reception than it deserved, though it is doubtful if any one of the rest took it as more than a basis for entertaining speculation. But, certainly, at this time their interest in the conditions they expected to find upon Mars became sharper.

Dale's anticipations were modest, but he admitted that he would be disappointed to find only a waterless world, incapable of supporting life, though he had started with just that expectation.

'You may have thought so,' the doctor said, 'but in reality that was just a check you put upon yourself to avoid the possibility of a painful disillusionment. You wouldn't have insisted on bringing me along as a biologist if you had no hope of finding any form of life. As I told you, I consider life as a stage in the decay of a planet, and I fully expect to find it. Probably it will have gone through the whole cycle and exist only in lowly forms as it did in the beginning, but it will surprise me very much if we find no living structures at all.'

'Pretty poor look out for me,' Froud thought. 'Depressing. Here's the world public, egged on by Burroughs and the rest into thinking that the place is crammed with weird animals, queer men and beautiful princesses, expecting me to go one better; and, according to you, I shall have to make thrilling, passionate romances out of the lives of a few amoebae and such-like. It's going to be hard work.'

Dugan looked at the doctor disappointedly.

'Do you really think it will be as dull as all that?

Surely life won't have sunk right to the limit. Won't there be animals of any kind?'

'Or crabs?' Froud added. 'Do you remember the monstrous crabs which Wells' time traveller found in the dying world? Nasty chaps—I used to dream about them when I was a kid. If there are many of them, I doubt whether my devoted public will get a story at all.'

The doctor shrugged.

'It's all guesswork. There may be only protozoa; there may be crustaceans——'

'And there are machines,' Joan said.

'Superb example of the one-track mind,' Froud remarked largely. 'I must say, I'm beginning to hope you're right; it'd give me plenty of material. But the point arises—who builds the machines? And what for? After all, as one of us said before, a machine is meant to *do* something.'

'If we could understand what machinery or The Machine implies,' Joan said, 'we might know more what to expect. Dale sees it as a work of art. His wife, from what he tells us, holds the very common opinion that it is opposed to art: that it stamps out individuality and personality. Dugan see it as a kind of huge plaything. Doctor Grayson'—she paused—'well, though you didn't actually say so, Doc, it seems to me that you are just content to use it because it is there. Like my father, you tend to disregard it and its effect except when you need to use it for practical ends?'

'Yes, I think that is fair. Man was not made for the machine: the machine was made for man to use or not, as he chooses.'

'And Froud's view of it is very little different, save that he is even more directly dependent on it for his living. But the fact remains that not one of you has really looked at the implications of the thing.'

'Don't get you. How does a machine "imply" anything?' Froud said.

'A machine doesn't. The existence of The Machine implies a great deal.

'Look here. Less than two centuries ago man began to

use power-driven machinery for the first time. There had, of course, been watermills, windmills and things driven by a horse going round in a circle, but they were not true ancestors of our machines, they were isolated discoveries, remaining essentially unchanged for centuries. When the power-driven machine arrived, it was something entirely *new* dropped into a world which was getting along quite well without it. Nobody saw its implications then beyond immediate profit, and they don't see them now. But we can look back over a hundred and fifty years and see what it has done.

'It was hailed as the creator of a new age, a kind of liberator of mankind, on one hand; and decried and frequently broken up by those who feared it as a competitor, on the other. Both of them were right, for it ultimately brought us leisure and a new world to enjoy in that leisure. The implication which everybody seems to have missed at the time was that those who would get a new world to enjoy and those who would get the leisure were not necessarily the same people.

'It seems to me as if at that stage of development a new Pandora's box was opened, and the whole human race was so excited at opening it that it took no precautions to net the troubles. The machine was just dropped into a world which was expected to go on working in the same old way as before. Obviously, it couldn't—any more than one's body could if the cook suddenly took to including large quantities of laxatives in every dish.

'Though it came as a slave, fifty years later it was the master. We had to support it in order that it might support us. The world population could not exist without it, and yet we had not learned to control it. It has given us innumerable blessings, and it has got us into countless messes—and still we cannot control it. We cannot predict more than its simplest and most obvious effects: and then we are often wrong.

'And now the machine is part of us, like our arms and legs—more important than either, for we couldn't even live if the machine were amputated from civilization.

'Yet we still have countless people who regard men

and machinery as separable. They think of the machine as a mere adjunct to life, something which gives faster communication, more production, more entertainment, still failing to see it as one of the great factors in our real lives, and not realizing that our people are as they are because of it. One hears of the Industrial Revolution as though it were a mere phase, finished and done with. It is not, and it shows no sign of ever being completed. And "Industrial Revolution!"—just as though it were like any little turn over of government. The machine came, and life could never be the same again: nor can it be static. But to what further changes is it leading us? That's what I mean by the implication of the machine.'

'I see,' the doctor said thoughtfully; 'then you think that if your ideas about the machine you found are right, we may be able to gather from Martian conditions some means of dealing with our own machine problems?'

Froud put in: 'Except that these comic, presumably Martian machines don't seem to be designed to *do* anything.'

'Yours is a pretty one-track mind on this subject, too,' the doctor told him, unkindly. 'You keep on saying that.'

'It's natural, isn't it? The first thing one wants to know about any machine is: "What is it for?" You can't get much further till you know that. The second is: "What makes it go?" and we've no answer to that, either.'

'As far as we are concerned,' Joan asked, 'does either of those questions matter as much as: "How did it become what it is?"'

'I don't know. I'm going to wait till I see one, and ask it—*if* I see one. The whole darned thing's too hypothetical for me,' Froud said shortly and, for him, unexpectedly.

Though there were times when the topic palled as indeed all topics palled, yet it remained frequently recurrent, and, becoming more accustomed, lost in the process much of its first fantastic quality. Familiarity admittedly breeds contempt where one's own preconceptions were at fault, but it is no less efficient at clearing up one's mental miscarriages. The occupants of the *Gloria Mundi* would have been surprised could they have made a direct comparison between their earlier defensive ridicule and the state of hypothetical acceptance which they gradually reached. The only one who yielded no ground either in conviction or assertion was Joan—unless that were also true of Burns.

But Burns was inscrutable. He had withdrawn into an aloofness which began to cause both the doctor and Dale serious misgiving. At times there was a look on his face and a curious glitter in his eyes which gave the former a very lively apprehension of trouble to come. Then he would sink back again into a less alarming, but no more healthy apathy from which it appeared impossible to rouse him. Since his frustrated assault upon Joan he had not troubled her actively. She could not decide in her own mind whether he was restrained by the thought of Froud's pistol which she habitually carried in her pocket, or by some mental process of his own. Nevertheless, she felt to some extent responsible for his isolation. Although she knew that Froud had not told the rest of the incident and that Burns' withdrawal was entirely voluntary, an instinct urged her to approach him and, if possible, draw him back into the party. For the first time she waived her resolution and singled one of the men out for special attention.

She took to including him pointedly in the general conversation; asking him questions unnecessarily to bring him out of his retirement. Frequently they remained unanswered, apparently unheard, and upon the occasion when he did reply, it was usually in monosyllables. But she persisted in spite of his stubbornness.

The climax came one 'day' over a month after they had passed the half-way stage. Under a fortnight now separated them from the end of the journey. An enlivened sense of expectation among the rest was making the engineer's isolation even more pronounced. Joan, feeling for some half-understood reason that the solidarity of the group was essential, sat down next to him and began to ask questions on the wear of rocket tube linings. The rest did not catch his reply, but they saw her stiffen and flush and noticed the gleam of anger in her eyes. Dugan chose to interfere. He walked across and demanded to know what Burns had said. Burns ignored him. Dugan repeated, angrily:

'What did you say to Miss Shirning just now?'

Burns looked up slowly. In his eyes was that expression which had worried the doctor, but he spoke calmly enough:

'You mind your own business.'

Dugan scowled, and looked questioningly at Joan. She shook her head.

'It was nothing,' she said.

Burns grinned unpleasantly.

'You see, she doesn't mind. And if you still want to know, I told her to stop bitching about here and to go and——'

But Dugan had his excuse. Before the engineer could finish, he had lunged at him. It was a clumsy stroke. Forgetful of his weightless condition, he misjudged it hopelessly. The blow missed the jaw and took the other on the shoulder; ineffectually, for his back was against the wall. Before any of the rest could interfere, Burns brought up one hard knobbly fist in a jolt to Dugan's chin, which broke the younger man's contact with the floor and sent him drifting obliquely upwards across the room. Burns laughed for the first time in weeks as the other struggled to make contact with his feet on the curved ceiling. Dugan, further infuriated by the sound, managed it at last. He turned, crouched a moment, and then launched himself back. But he did not reach the engineer. Dale and Froud, by common consent, intercepted his flight and dragged him to the floor.

Froud has since been heard to lament the necessity. A fight unhampered by gravity promised to be a uniquely interesting spectacle, but he agreed with Dale that it could not be risked.

Joan moved away from Burns whose grin grew the more sardonic as he watched her go. Froud and Dale hung on to Dugan while his anger cooled into sullenness. The little flare was allowed to fade into unsatisfactory inconclusiveness, but it left behind it an increased hostility between the participants, and an increased misgiving among the rest. The gap between them and the engineer, already too wide, was enlarged.

'Not long now,' said the doctor.

He and Joan were standing beside one of the windows. The pink disc had swelled to about the size of the full moon seen from Earth. It seemed to hang a little above them, looking only just out of reach. One would have only to be a little taller, it seemed, to stretch out and pluck the shining ball from the sky. It was so near now, and yet mysterious and secret as ever.

So puzzling, too, with its criss-cross markings which might be canals, its white-capped poles which almost certainly were ice-bound. The telescopic instruments had told them scarcely anything, for it proved to be exasperatingly impossible to keep them trained steadily upon one spot. Froud was sure that he had seen a glint of water in one of the dark markings, but no one could support him. The doctor claimed to have caught a glimpse of a stone formation which could not be natural, but it had been no more than a glimpse, and he had been unable to pick it up again. The rest had distinguished nothing.

'Only four days more,' the doctor amplified.

'An age. Four of the longest days I shall ever spend,' she said, without turning. 'Somehow, now that we are so near, I'm afraid. For the first time I am beginning to doubt whether it ever really happened. Suppose it was all a dream—that the machine never really existed at all ...' Her voice trailed away. They gazed up at the planet in silence for some minutes before she went on:

'If it isn't true—if they're right after all, and Mars is only a dead world with nothing left, or if it has not even lived, what shall I do? I can't go back and face them ... I couldn't face any of you ... I'll kill myself.'

It was her first sign of weakness. Her first admission of the questioning doubt which had nagged more and more insistently during the last weeks. Suppose after all that they had been wrong? That she and her father had been cruelly hoaxed? No, that was impossible. Such a machine could not have been built on Earth, and yet . . .

The doctor had turned away from the window and was watching her closely.

'That's not like you,' he said, with a frown. 'You've not been sleeping properly lately.'

'Not much,' she admitted. 'It's this getting so close, and yet not knowing any more than when we left. Suppose . . .'

'You've got to stop supposing. You're getting edgy, and that's no help to any of us. Let me give you some stuff.'

'All right.' She nodded wearily. 'But not just yet. Let me watch a little longer.'

He grunted. 'There's nothing to see yet. Old Mars is keeping his secrets well.'

'I'm afraid,' Joan repeated. 'If I was right—if that machine was an individual, what does it mean? What are we going to meet there? How are they likely to deal with us? It frightens me, Doc. Inhuman machines . . .'

He took her by the arm. 'This sort of thing won't do, Joan. You're working yourself up to no purpose. I'll give you that sedative.'

'Yes.' She smiled ruefully. 'This isn't like me, is it? I'm sorry. You won't tell the others?'

'I won't—if you'll take the stuff right away. A good long sleep'll do you a world of good. Make you see everything differently. Come along.'

Dale fastened the safety-belt and anchored himself into the control seat.

'Shutters closed,' he ordered.

The great curve of the planet now occupied half the field of view, and it was with reluctance that his crew withdrew to swing the shutters across.

'We can afford to slow up more gently than we accelerated,' Dale told them. 'In fact, we'll have to, because I've got to see where we're going. Now, couches everyone.'

'How I hate that order,' murmured the doctor, as he obeyed and fastened his straps, this time unaided.

'Ready? Here goes then,' Dale said.

He pushed forward his lever. The *Gloria Mundi* quivered throughout her structure. The droning roar of the rocket tubes grew louder. Bodies that had been weightless for nearly three months felt a curious sense of heaviness descend upon them. The pressure increased, the more unpleasant for its unfamiliarity. The speed indicator began to back to less fantastic figures as they approached on a spiral which took advantage of the planet's rotation. Two thousand miles above the surface Dale found that his ship was still going too fast. He advanced the lever farther.

'Ugh,' grunted Froud. 'Happy landing,' he muttered, before he gave himself up to contemplation of his own discomfort.

The power of the rocket discharges increased. The passengers' symptoms became unpleasantly like those attending their start.

CHAPTER XIV

BURNS PLAYS A HAND

THE *Gloria Mundi* landed close to one of the vegetation belts which wrap Mars in a large meshed web. Inevitably she toppled on her side, rolling and bumping as she slithered to a final stop. She came to rest with two of her windows buried in the sand and another staring straight up into a purplish-blue sky. But the time Joan managed to crawl from her couch back into the main room, the shutters on the other two windows had been swung back and a jostling was going on for vantage-points. The doctor surrendered his place to her, and withdrew. It was his job, in his capacity of the expedition's chemist, to analyse a sample of the atmosphere.

Joan gazed upon a Martian landscape for the first time. And she was disappointed. So poor a climax it looked for so much endurance. In spite of reason, their subconscious expectations had been higher, or, at least, different. Now that they saw what had been foretold, she, and Dugan beside her, felt let down.

It was a desert. A vista of reddish rocks and drifted sand, arid and hot, extending to the limits of their view. A dreary waste upon which nothing moved or grew; where the sun caught in glittering points upon harsh crystalline fragments, emphasizing its inhospitality. Her spirits fell. Such a land could produce nothing, nothing at all. They had been right, those who had said that Mars was only a lifeless globe. Perhaps life, after all, was just an accident which had happened once . . .

Then it was borne in upon her that Dale and Froud at the other window were exclaiming excitedly. Even Burns was contributing a few sentences. She hurried across the floor (which had been the wall when the rocket was erect) and joined them.

Stunted, rusty-looking bushes of unfamiliar shapes dotted the sand at some distance from this side of the ship, stragglers from a main front of vegetation which began about a mile away. Poor stuff it was, scraggy and parched and brittle in appearance, but it represented life. The bushes had evolved here, what else might not have arisen? And they still lived. The planet was not yet dead while sap still flowed, however thinly through those twisted stems and coppery, spade-shaped leaves which fluttered a little in the breeze. The sight which excited the rest into exclamations, kept her silent.

The doctor's voice suddenly drew their attention. He had made his tests of the atmosphere.

'The components,' he was saying, 'seem to be much the same as our own, and not in very different proportions, save for a lower percentage of carbon dioxide. It will be perfectly safe for us to breathe it, but the pressure is considerably less than our accustomed fifteen pounds, so that it will be necessary for us to wear oxygen masks to supplement it. You will all be relieved to hear that we shall not have to use the cumbrous space suits, but, in view of the high temperature in the sun, we shall have to wear heat-insulated overalls.'

There was a rush for the lockers, and a babble of talk as they pulled on the stiff overalls.

'Thank God we've not got to use the space suits,' said Froud. 'Not only do they smell abominably, but it's quite impossible for a bloke to show the dignity proper to Earth's ambassadors when he's dressed up like a cross between a deep-sea diver and an Eskimo. Not, of course, that we'll look any too handsome in oxygen masks, but we'll be able to give them a suggestion of the true human shape.'

Joan was wrestling with one of the spare overall suits which was several times too large for her.

'Well, none of your machines has come to look us up yet,' Dale said, as he adjusted the oxygen pack over his shoulder-blades.

'You wait a bit.' She attempted a light tone. 'They'll turn up. It's not likely that a thing like the *Gloria Mundi* can have come roaring into Martian skies quite unnoticed.'

'If there's anything beyond a lot of mangy-looking bushes to notice her,' he answered sceptically.

'Give them time,' she said.

'Quite,' the doctor agreed. 'You can't expect them to just pop up from the ground. If they exist at all, we don't know how far they may have to come. This doesn't look like a residential district even for machines. By the way, where are we?'

'Bit north of the equator. That's as much as I can tell you.' Dale crossed to a locker. As he opened it, he said: 'Everyone is to take a rifle and a belt of ammunition. I know it may seem a ridiculous thing to do, but re-member that we know nothing at all about this place. Appearances may be quite deceptive.'

'What? Me, too?' Froud expostulated. 'But, look here, what with movie-cameras and still-cameras and whatnot, I'm going to look like a bazaar and exchange column already. Have a heart.'

'They don't weigh as much here as they do at home,' was Dale's only consolation. 'We can't afford to take any risks. Where life is possible for bushes, it's quite likely to be possible for other things.'

'Ah, the Wellsian crabs again.'

'We'll see. In any case, nobody is to split off from the rest until we know a bit more. That clear? We keep together.'

He dealt out the light rifles and bandoliers and waited while they were slung. There was a further delay while Froud attached to himself camera-cases, stand-holders, light-meters, extra lens carriers, etc. At last:

'Behold! The human Christmas Tree,' he said.

Dale saw to the adjustments of the masks and tubes which fed oxygen through the nose, leaving the mouth free. When he was assured that they were all working properly, he crossed to the entrance port and for the first time in the seventy-four days since they had left Earth, swung it open. One by one he passed his crew through the airlock.

Joan, the last to emerge, save for Dale himself, crossed the coarse, reddish sand to Froud's side. He was taking a series of snapshots of the uninspiring view.

'Martian idea of a landscape—pretty inferior,' he said, conversationally. 'I must say this place is something of a flop. We've got deserts every bit as good at home, and no need to dress up for them. Now I suppose I had better take a shot or two of the old *G.M.*, to be entitled: "Earth's Adventurers at Their Goal," or "The Triumph of——" '

'Shush!' said Joan.

'What do you mean: "shush"?'

She nudged him, and nodded towards the entrance port. Dale had just left the airlock; in one hand he carried a trowel, and in the other, a rod with a flag attached to it. The rest watched while he dug a small hole, planted his pole, and stamped the red sand back about its base. He stood back. The Union Jack unfolded gently in the light Martian breeze. Dale saluted.

'In the name of Her Majesty Queen Elizabeth the Second of England, I proclaim this land a part of the British Commonwealth of Nations. In her name, and in the name of all the peoples of the Commonwealth, I honour the brave men who gave their lives that this thing might be done. To their memory let it be dedicated, to their glory let it thrive. They gave us this land, not in bloodshed, but with their life's blood. May we prove worthy of their trust.'

In the silence which followed an air of constraint fell over the party. The doctor looked a little quizzically at Dale and then let his gaze wander to the journalist. But Froud did not catch his eye. True to his training, he was apparently interested only in providing a record of the occasion, and all his attention was engaged by the manipulation of a small movie-camera.

Dale finished his ceremony.

'What now?' Dugan asked, breaking the silence self-consciously.

'That seems to be the only way worth looking,' Froud said. He pointed towards the bushes. The doctor agreed:

'I must have some specimens of those; the sooner the better.'

'All right.' Dale produced a small compass. 'Heaven knows where the magnetic centre of this place is, but it's got one somewhere, luckily. If we assume that it is in the north it will give us something to go by. That means that the bushes are due west. Don't forget what I said about keeping together.'

The thicker vegetation, when they reached it, proved to be much the same as the stunted bushes in all except size. Before long, it became clear that the party, with the exception of the doctor, was unspokenly endorsing Froud's opinion of the red planet. The twisted stems of the bushes were hollow and so brittle as to prove no obstacle. Their advance was accompanied by a sharp crackling of broken branches mingled with the papery rustling of the subsiding foliage, but the view of brown thickets continuously before them was as monotonous as the desert behind them.

After half an hour's progress, the only member of the band who did not feel that attainment can be the most potent source of dissatisfaction was the doctor. With what seemed to be a singularly slight supply of fuel he managed to keep his botanical fervour at high pressure, continually causing delays by his determination to secure a specimen which, to the inexpert eye, showed no difference from the many shoots, leaves, branches and roots he had already put in his boxes.

The vegetation belts bordering the Martian canals vary in width according to the nature of the soil. In satisfactorily porous regions they may extend as far as twenty miles to either side, but in others they dwindle into desert at no more than a mile or two from the bank. It was owing to the chance which had landed the *Gloria Mundi* beside one of the narrower fertile strips that her crew was able to notice a change in the condition of the plants when they had covered a little more than a mile. The bushes, though at first unchanged in type, were healthier and better nourished. It became a little less easy for them to force their way through. Moister stems bent more and broke less easily. Moreover, to the doctor's delight, a few new variations were to be seen farther on. He pounced with enthusiasm upon a number of bulbous, olive-brown plants not unlike spineless cacti, and held forth with an excitement which left the rest cold.

'Look like old leather bags to me,' Froud told him. 'How much farther into this not so virgin forest do you propose to lead us?' he added disconsolately to Dale.

'A bit farther yet,' Dale told him. 'Doc's got to get all the odds and ends he can, and it looks as if there might be more variety ahead.'

As they continued, now with little enthusiasm, an uphill slope of the ground became increasingly perceptible. Almost another mile must have been covered when Dale stopped suddenly and held up his hand. They stopped wonderingly in a silence broken only by the rubbing together of the harsh stems and a flutter of leaves.

'What is it?' Joan asked.

Dale relaxed his listening attitude.

'I thought I heard something ahead—a sort of clanking noise. Didn't anyone else?'

They shook their heads, and he owned that he might have been mistaken. But, in spite of his words, his manner was more cautious as they went on and the rest caught from it a sense of expectation. A little later it was Joan who stopped them with a sudden command:

'Listen!'

But again the silence remained unbroken save by natural stirrings.

'What's the idea?' Froud inquired. 'Are you trying to make it more exciting by putting the wind up us ...?'

'Shut up!' snapped Dale.

Faintly, but quite unplaceably, the whole party distinguished a sound of crackling somewhere not far away. Without a word, Dale unslung his rifle and released the safety-catch. He moved ahead, holding it ready. But whatever had been responsible for the sound was not in his path, nor did it betray its presence again. Nevertheless:

'This place doesn't seem to be quite empty, after all,' Dugan said. 'It must have been something pretty big.'

As the bushes became stronger and higher and the going more difficult, Dale took the lead, and they fell without prearrangement into single file. The ground changed its character, becoming softer and less desiccated. Before long, Dale was calling back that it was lighter ahead, and a few minutes later, they emerged into the open. In the astonished silence Dugan said:

'I suppose this *is* a canal, and not a sea?'

To both right and left the bank stretched away in an unbroken line. In front, the water reached to the horizon, ruffled lightly by the breeze, and sparkling in the sunlight. Dale tasted the water and spat it out again; it was brackish.

'All the same, it's one of the canals. They're a good

many miles wide, remember, even the smallest of them.'

'And the horizon's closer than it is at home,' the doctor put in. 'It's almost incredible that they should have been made artificially—and we don't seem to be much closer to knowing who or what made them. The slope we've been climbing must have been the stuff which they——'

'Look! What's that?' Dugan cried in sudden excitement.

He was pointing away to the left. A dark object, difficult to make out at such a distance, was pushing its way through the water. A fleck of white at the nearer end suggested a low bow wave. Dale pulled out his field-glasses.

'What is it?' Froud asked, striving to erect a tripod and change the lens of his camera simultaneously. 'Coming this way?'

'Can't see. There's not much of it above the water-line. Shaped something like a whale. Seems to be going due south.'

'Here, let me look.' The doctor almost snatched the glasses and hurriedly refocused. But he could make out no more. It was even impossible for him to decide whether he was looking at a living creature or a form of vessel. He swore fluently.

'How about letting off a few shots to attract its attention,' Dugan suggested. But Dale disapproved.

'No, there's no telling what that might let us in for—and we're a good distance from the *Gloria Mundi*. It'll be better to go a bit cautiously till we know more.'

Froud had set up his small camera behind an enormous lens, and was hopefully taking a series of pictures, with Dale, Dugan and the doctor standing beside him, straining their eyes to catch more details. An exclamation behind them caused all four to turn at once.

Burns was facing them. His left arm was around Joan's waist, holding her with her back pressed against his chest. In his right hand he held a pistol.

Dale frowned and his eyes narrowed; he opened his lips to speak, but changed his mind. The look on the engineer's face warned him to be cautious. With an effort he cleared his frown; his voice sounded almost casual as he asked:

'Hullo, what's the trouble, Burns?'

At the same time he kept his eyes on the girl's face, trying to convey by his attitude that she could behave calmly. It seemed that she understood, for he noticed that she relaxed a trifle, but he had reckoned without his companions.

'What the hell do you think you're doing? Take your hands off her, damn you,' Dugan shouted.

He stepped forward with his fists clenched.

'Get back,' snapped the engineer. 'Get back, or I'll drill you.'

There could be no doubt that he meant it. Dugan hesitated and then sullenly retreated. Froud yawned.

'What's all this about? It seems very dramatic,' he remarked.

Burns turned his attention from Dugan and glared at the journalist.

'And don't you be too free with your words. I owe you something, don't forget. You know what it's about, all right; you all know, damn well. Do you think I didn't know what was going on all the way here? Do you think I don't know why I wasn't wanted? You've all had your fun, damn you, now I'm going to have mine.'

Froud assumed an expression of puzzlement.

'Do you mean——?'

'Shut up, you.'

'But, look here, Burns, you're making a mistake, you know——' Dale began in reasonable tones.

'Oh, I am, am I? I'd be making a big one if I believed you. You! I suppose you think I didn't see the way you changed to her after you'd had her?'

'Damn you. I didn't——'

'Oh, so you didn't?—and I suppose the rest of you didn't either? What do you think I am—blind? To hell with the ruddy lot of you. I saw you all sneaking off to the storeroom different times. Having her as you wanted and leaving me out as if I wasn't human. And thinking

I'd stand for it. Well, I did—but I'm not doing it any longer. It's my turn now. And there's not going to be any sharing.'

'But, man, you've got it all wrong——' the doctor put in. 'We didn't——'

'That's right. Back one another up, but you're not going to fool me. I've been waiting for this. Thinking of it for weeks. I admit that you did fool me at first—seeing that you're old enough to be her father—but not for long. And now it's my turn.'

'You damn' swine. That girl——'

Burns swung his pistol.

'That'll be enough from you, Dugan. Keep your mouth shut.'

Dale looked at the engineer steadily. He was wondering whether he could risk a shot. His rifle was loaded and ready in his hands, but he knew that it would be tricky work to avoid hitting Joan. Burns, with his handier weapon, would most likely fire before he himself could aim. He exchanged a helpless glance with the doctor.

Burns turned his pistol so that its muzzle was pressed into the girl's side.

'If I don't have her, nobody has her,' he said. 'Now you put your rifles down over there'—he nodded at a spot half-way between himself and them—'one by one, or something very nasty is going to happen.'

They hesitated, but the look in Burns' eyes was dangerous; he was not out to bluff.

'Come on,' he snapped.

Froud shrugged his shoulders, walked slowly forward, laid his rifle down at the place indicated, and stepped back. The doctor followed, then Dale, and, finally, Dugan.

Burns nodded. 'Now get back, all of you. Right back to the water.'

They did as he ordered, and he walked to the rifles, still holding the girl.

'Pick them up,' he ordered her.

Joan obeyed. The pistol pressed into her side gave her

no option. She did not for a moment doubt that he would use it if necessary; she appreciated no less than the rest that in his present crazed, inflamed condition he was capable of anything. The pistol which Froud had given her was in her pocket, but the pocket was hopelessly out of reach beneath the stiff overalls. Even had it been handy, she doubted her ability to seize it and get in the first shot. One by one she handed the rifles to Burns and he, transferring the pistol from one hand to the other, slung them over his shoulders.

'And your own,' he said cuttingly. 'Don't forget that.'

She slipped it off her own shoulder and handed it across. He looked at the four men thoughtfully and then dropped his eyes to his own pistol. It was an unpleasant moment.

'No,' he decided, 'no sense in wasting good bullets. But if any of you are thinking of following us—just think again, that's my advice.'

His large hand closed on the girl's arm. He grinned unattractively.

'Say good-bye to your lovers,' he told her.

'You——' Dugan began.

Burns jerked his pistol round. There was a sharp crack and a spurt of dirt at Dugan's feet.

'Next time it'll be higher,' he said.

He left them without another word. Casting frequent glances over his shoulder, he led the girl back by the way they had come.

CHAPTER XV

—AND IS TRUMPED

THE four who remained watched Burns and Joan disappear into the bushes. It was some time before anyone spoke. Froud sat down on the ground, dismantling his camera and folding up its stand. The rest stood watching him. At the moment there seemed to be nothing to be said. It was Dugan who asked the question which the rest had thought not worth putting into words.

'Well,' he said harshly, 'aren't we going to do something?'

'Not yet,' Dale told him briefly. Dugan stared.

'What's wrong with you? If you're not going to help that girl, I am.'

He turned and ran towards the bushes.

'Come back, you fool,' Dale called, but Dugan took no notice. He disppeared at a trot in Burns' track. A moment later came the sharp crack of a shot. The three men looked at one another, but Dugan reappeared. He returned looking shaken and not a little sheepish.

'Felt the wind of it,' he said.

'You were lucky,' Dale told him. 'Now sit down and behave as though you were grown up.'

'This,' said Froud, digging one hand beneath his overalls, 'is a mess.' His fumbling ceased and he produced a yellow packet. 'Have a cigarette.'

Each of them took one. He lit one, and pulled a wry face. 'My God, how beastly! That's what three months' abstinence does for you.'

'What,' Dugan asked again, but less heatedly than before, 'are we going to do about it?'

'Nothing,' Dale told him.

'Nothing? You mean——'

The doctor laid his hand on Dugan's arm.

'Quietly, lad. You don't see what the trouble is. What you're wanting now is a good stand-up fight with a man whom you consider a swine.'

'Well, isn't he?'

'May be, but the point is that for the moment, at least, he isn't sane. I've been watching him these last few weeks—perhaps it is my fault in a way that this has happened: I ought to have warned you all that he was on the edge. But I counted on our arrival here having a normalizing effect; I was wrong. He isn't responsible, and in his present state you couldn't help doing more harm than good: he'd kill her rather than let any of us get near, of that I'm certain. In fact, I'm surprised he didn't shoot us as we stood.'

'So am I,' Froud agreed. 'And I had a nasty, clammy idea that he might hit on the idea of letting out our oxygen supply—By the way, Dale, how long is it good for?'

'With careful use, at the present rate, it might last twenty hours, I think.'

'Of which two have gone already.'

'And you mean we're to do nothing?' Dugan repeated, still incredulous.

'The only person who can do anything is that girl,' the doctor said. 'And, if I know Joan, she will. I've got faith in her, and she knows how the situation stands, all right.'

'But suppose we were to cut quickly through the bushes parallel with him and ambush him at the other end?'

'What! With those leaves making a noise like a whole brown-paper factory? Have some sense,' Froud said. 'No, Doc's is the idea. She's got a pistol, and she'll get a chance to use it sooner or later.'

'And if she doesn't?'

'Then it's a poor look out for us. I suppose Burns will just sit comfortably in the *G.M.* and watch us pass out from suffocation.'

'But what good's that going to do him? He can't take the *G.M.* back alone.'

'Can't you get it into your nut that the man isn't sane any longer? All he wants at the moment is the girl, and revenge on us because he supposes we left him out—he isn't thinking of himself beyond that.'

Dugan frowned worriedly. 'Yes *I* see that now, but do you really think *she* does? I mean, suppose she lets it go until too late, expecting us to take a hand——?'

'She won't.'

But though Froud sounded definite, he was by no means convinced in his own mind. *If* Joan could shoot Burns, all would be well. But could she? A second's hesitation at the critical moment might give him the chance to disarm her. A trembling of her hand or any slight misjudgment might only result in an infuriating flesh wound. It was not an easy thing to shoot down even a madman in cold blood. Did she, after all, fully realize what was going to happen to her—and to all of them—if she were to let an opportunity slip?

Conversation languished. Each of the four sat silently considering unpleasant possibilities.

'How long are you giving him, Dale?' the doctor asked, at last.

'I thought an hour. It's difficult to tell. For all we know, he may still be waiting for us round the first corner.'

The other nodded. An hour, he thought, should give them a good margin, provided they went cautiously. He doubted whether a man in Burns' state of mind would have the patience to lie long in ambush.

Dale rose when the time was up.

'Now, remember, go as quietly as you can. And we're not going to hurry. Caution's a damn' sight more important than speed just now. Our game is to be near when something happens, but we don't want to make it happen.'

They had covered perhaps a third of the distance to the rocket when there came the sharp, unmistakable sound of a rifle-shot ahead. Dale, in the lead, stopped dead, listening. There was a second shot, followed by several more in rapid succession. Dale broke into a clumsy run, keeping his feet with difficulty against the low gravity which threw him into a series of striding leaps. The rest followed as well as they were able. If it did cross Dale's mind that this might be a trap cunningly contrived for them, he took no notice of the idea. Undoubtedly there had been things other than themselves moving in the bushes. It looked as if Burns had discovered what those things were.

They found him no great way from the edge of the desert. His body lay in the centre of the track, face to the sky. It was nasty. Of the girl there was no sign.

The four stopped abruptly. The sight was sickening.

'Good God,' said Froud. 'What can have done that?'

He looked nervously about him. There was no hint of anything lurking in the bushes, no sound but the fretting together of the dried stems and whispering rustle of the leaves. Yet a short while ago something had been here—something big and dangerous. The doctor knelt down without a word. He raised the trampled and broken body, slipped the rifle slings from the shoulders and handed the weapons back to their owners. There were six among the four of them. Dugan took two. Dale bent down and eased his second out of the dead hands. Its magazine was empty. He reloaded before he spoke. The rest waited for him with their eyes restlessly searching the thickets and the rifles ready in their hands.

'She may have run on to the ship,' he said. 'We'd better look. Later, when we know what we are up against, we'll come back for poor Burns.'

They went on. Slowly this time. Doing their best to minimize the crackling of each step. They explored the meshed bushes around them with apprehensive glances, fearful of seeing an unexpected movement. But still nothing showed and no suspicious sound came to their ears.

The vegetation became shorter and sparser, and they knew with relief that they were nearing the desert once more. Once on the open sand they would be safe from a surprise attack. In the tall scrub the advantage lay overwhelmingly with the attacker. A hundred yards more and they had reached the edge. The taller growths gave way quite abruptly to the little, knee-high withered shrubs. Beyond lay the rolling dunes of reddish sand and occasional outcrops of rock, and across them they could see the *Gloria Mundi* a-glitter with slanting rays of the sun. An audible sigh of relief rose from all four of the men.

'I don't know what I've been waiting for, but thank God it hasn't happened,' said Froud.

'There are rare times when we are in complete agreement,' the doctor admitted.

'What was that?' Dugan said sharply.

'What was what?'

'I saw something flash, close to the *G.M.*'

'Probably Joan showing she's seen us,' Froud suggested. 'I expect she's—yes, there it is again.'

'Damn. I must have left my glasses by the water,' Dale said.

'Well, we're certainly not going back to fetch them, so let's get on.'

They had covered half the distance when Dale called another halt.

'It seems to me I can see things moving just by her,' he said.

'You're right,' Dugan agreed. 'But I can't make out what they are. Do you think——'

'Look!' cried the doctor. His voice held a panicky sound which made them spin round.

Emerging from the bushes they had just left was a procession which left them speechless.

Dale alone kept his presence of mind. Close beside them was a small hillock of broken rocks and drifted sand. He gave the order to run for it.

'And hold your fire till I give the word,' he added, as they flung themselves flat upon the top.

CHAPTER XVI

JOAN STARTS A JOURNEY

JOAN, who was in front, had been the first to see the thing. They were in a hurry—at least, Burns was, and, in the circumstances, that meant that she was, too. He had waited just long enough to fire the single warning shot which had sent Dugan back to the rest before urging her swiftly on their way. His manner had changed. With the others safely out of sight, his confidence became displaced by a nervous anxiety to put the stout hull of the *Gloria Mundi* between himself and dangers known or unknown as soon as possible. She noticed, moreover, that he had put his pistol back in his pocket, and was holding one of the rifles ready for an emergency. The altered attitude increased her nervousness of the surroundings, but it made him seem more normal. And his eyes no longer held that cruel gleam which had made her feel weak almost to the point of panic.

As they hurried on, her thoughts ran ahead. She had nothing to fear from him now, until they reached the rocket. But once inside it, with the outer door closed . . .? They would take off their oxygen masks. Then the padded overalls. She would have a chance to reach the pistol in her pocket—That was it. While he was struggling out of his protective suit, her chance would come. It would put him at her mercy for a few necessary moments. And there must be no mistake. For the sake of the rest as well as for herself she could risk no mistake. . . .

The bushes around them were drier now; the ground underfoot, sandier. Quite soon they would reach the open desert. It would not take long to reach—— Then she had seen it. A glimpse of something glittering bluely which moved in the bushes to the right. She swerved wildly away from it. A kind of jointed rod swept out from it, barely missing her arm, and a sudden terror seemed to stab her in the chest. She sprang forward, running and leaping without daring to look behind. She heard Burns' cry of surprise. There was the sound of a shot and then of a fusillade as the automatic rifle emptied itself. The noise drove her on faster. There was a cry, like a thin scream behind her, and terror seemed to give her wings so that she flew through the bushes. She never looked back.

Then the bushes abruptly finished and she stumbled out among the little wizened shrubs. But she did not check her headlong flight. She had no intention of stopping before the *Gloria Mundi*'s door was safely shut between her and whatever had been in the bushes. Not until she was half-way across the sand did she catch sight of the things which were moving around the rocket. Then, in dismay, she checked herself. She could not risk going on to meet them, but she dared not face the bushes again. There was nothing for it, but to wait where she was. Dale and the rest must have heard the shots; they would be here soon. She looked round, searching for a hollow where she could lie hidden until they should come.

A sudden glitter on top of one of the rocky ridges away to her right caught her eye. She started, looking more attentively. It flashed again, without any doubt the reflection from a swiftly moving metal object. She stood rigidly watching it as it approached rapidly. Each time it breasted a ridge or a sandy hummock she could distinguish more details. Soon there could be no doubt that it was the counterpart of the machine in her photographs—with the difference that it scurried along on six legs instead of eight. Joan stood, waiting for it.

At twenty yards' distance it stopped and turned its lenses on her. A series of sounds in metallic timbre came from one of the openings in its casing. In the thin air they sounded harsh and attenuated. Joan, after a moment's hesitation, advanced to a smooth patch of sand and wrote there a few characters with her forefinger. Then she stood back and waited.

The machine approached with no sound but the thudding of its six feet on the sand. It stopped close to the scratched characters, examining them carefully. Joan had written that she came from Earth, and peacefully.

Again the metallic tones issued from its speaker. She smoothed the sand and began to write again.

'Write. I cannot understand speech.'

One of the machine's four tentacles whipped forward. it scrawled swiftly:

'How do you know our writing?'

Laboriously, compared with the machine's swift action, Joan drew her reply.

'A machine came to Earth.'

'Did it bring you? Where is it?' scribbled the machine.

'No, it was'—she hesitated—'broken,' she finished.

She watched it as it began to write again. Suddenly, with no more than three characters completed, it stopped. Before she could guess its intention it had dashed forward. Two of the metal tentacles wrapped round her and lifted her. A third flashed out, striking at something behind her, and meeting it with a clang. Held as she was, she could not see what threatened. She was only aware of a jointed metal arm which whipped past her head and fell with a harmless clatter on the case of the machine which held her. The surprise was so complete; the action so unexpected as utterly to bewilder her. The next thing she knew was that she was travelling across the desert in the grasp of a machine which sped at a prodigious pace towards the south.

CHAPTER XVII

MAKING ACQUAINTANCES

THE four men lying prone on the top of the sandhill watched the string of metal machines which had emerged from the scrub. The creation which Joan's photographs had shown them had seemed weird, but these newcomers were a nightmare. They all felt a hysterical disbelief of their own senses: the things they saw must be a hallucination. Dugan, with an attempt at light-heartedness, said:

'I know what is is. Someone's been putting alcohol in my air supply.' But his intended nonchalance was belied by the tremor in his voice.

Froud blinked at the mechanical cavalcade. He shook his head decidedly.

'I'm sorry, but I just don't believe it,' he said.

No two of the machines were alike. They differed in shape, size and form both of their main casings and of their appendages. Some were spherical bodied, some cubical, some pyramidal, some rectangular and a few of the roughly coffin shape that Joan had described to them. The only point which they all held in common was that each moved upon struts of one kind or another; not a wheel was to be seen. Froud stared particularly at one egg-shaped monstrosity. It was supported on one side by two long jointed stilts which were splayed out widely to compensate for the three scurrying, but far shorter legs on the other side. Another, a torpedo-like contrivance, had only one leg on either side at the rear and upheld its forepart on a kind of skid. One of the spheres managed to get along on a tripod of unequal struts, clanking and clattering as it lurched about. Many of the cases were discoloured by smears of a kind of rust and patched in places with plates of non-matching metals; here and there one could see parts which had been painted, but not one of the machines was the same colour all over.

'Crazy, crazy, crazy. It can't be real,' Froud repeated.

'If I read of this, I should throw the book away,' said the doctor. 'But it exists; it's real. There must be some kind of reason for it somewhere.'

The ungainly machines spread out into a crescent formation and continued to approach, the faster reducing their speeds to the lumbering pace of the slower.

'When I give the word,' Dale said. 'Aim for their lenses—and go easy on the bullets, we've got none to waste.'

'I suppose they *are* hostile,' Froud put in; 'but you remember what Joan said——'

'These aren't the things she talked about. Besides, I'm remembering what Burns looked like, and not taking any chances,' Dale said.

He waited patiently. They were within sixty yards when he gave the order to fire.

The result of the first volley was unexpectedly gratifying. The advance stopped dead. One machine dropped to the ground with its metal legs splayed out around it. Another burst into fragments with a surprising concussion. A third ran amuck. It staggered, turned half round, then with tentacles flailing wildly and a great clanking proceeding from its loosely articulated parts, it set off drunkenly over the desert as fast as five ill-matched legs could carry it. Dale gave the order for a second round.

One more machine fell. The legs of a second jammed so that it ploughed round in a circle. The undamaged machines began to retire, dragging the injured with them. Froud dropped his rifle and seized a camera.

'Study of a flock of Whathaveyous in full retreat,' he murmured.

'She was right about one thing—they can think,' the doctor said. 'They're not just remote control mechanisms—they're intelligent, self-contained machines.'

'Maybe,' Froud grunted, 'but it seems to me precious like the kind of intelligence you find in mental homes. And I feel a bit that way myself. Damn it all, it can't be real—even here. It's—it's a kind of dream made of Lewis Carroll and Karel Capek rolled together. There's no sense in machines like this. Just look at 'em. What the hell's the good of 'em?'

'Yes, but remember the one in Joan's photographs. It was all right. Queer as it looked to us, it was at least logically designed and all of a piece. Something's gone wrong with these. They aren't reasonable—sort of crazy bad jokes. Look at that square chap.'

He pointed at one of the cubes. From its lower corners sprang two well-paired metal legs and one entirely dissimilar leg, while the fourth was upheld by a flexible tentacle. It was busily engaged in dragging away one of the broken machines by means of other tentacles protruding from three of its upper corners.

'I've got an idea about that. Keep your eye on it for a bit,' advised Dale.

When it had reached what it evidently considered a safe distance, the cube stopped; a lens set in one of its sides was brought to bear, and it probed inquisitively about in the wreckage. Apparently satisfied, it lowered its own casing to the ground and began industriously to dismember the other machine. Five minutes later it stood erect again, but with a difference. It rested now upon four legs and four tentacles waved from its top corners. By taking a leg from its wrecked companion, it had been enabled to shift the jury-leg tentacle back to its rightful position. Now, apart from minor discrepancies in the length of the legs, it was complete and ready for anything.

'Well, that settles it. We're all quite mad,' said Froud.

'Queer,' muttered the doctor, 'indecent, too, somehow. —A kind of mechanical cannibalism.'

He watched another machine with ludicrously ill-assorted members approach the casualty and exchange a badly damaged tentacle for one in better condition.

'Do you suppose that the ultimate is a kind of super monster built entirely of spare parts?'

'Don't ask me anything,' Froud told him. 'I'm still feeling as if my middle name were Alice.'

The surviving machines having stripped the fallen of all useful parts reformed their ranks and began to advance again.

'Same as before,' Dale ordered.

The second repulse was almost a duplication of the first.

'It's easy. We'll be all right as long as the shots and the air hold out,' he decided, 'but God knows what's happened to Joan.'

Joan's captor sped over the desert with scarcely a sound save the scraping of its metal feet on the coarse sand and an occasional clink as they struck fragments of stone. Only the faintest low-pitched hum told of the machinery at work within the casing; machinery which was acting with a flawless accuracy and judgment beyond the capacity of any animal creation. Not once did it hesitate and not once did it err in placing the six hurrying legs. The smooth, relentless perfection of its progress over the rough ground was uncanny; every climb and every descent was made without a suggestion of a slip or stumble.

After her first shock she had struggled desperately, but, held as she was, it was impossible for her to reach the pocket where her pistol lay. In her panic she battered on the casing until her hands became sore even in their thick gloves, but upon the machine it had no effect whatever. After that, she relapsed into a fatalistic acceptance of the situation. At the rate they had travelled it would take her hours to find her way back over the desert. As far as she could, she resigned herself to face whatever fate the machine intended for her.

Once in the journey she had caught sight of a group of machines to the west: and they had seen her captor, too. They came scuttering awkwardly but speedily to investigate. Her machine swerved and put on speed. It left them behind easily. But the sight of them bewildered her even as, had she known it, a similar sight was bewildering Dale and the rest. The queer, distorted mechanisms which she had glimpsed did not fit in at all with the logical world she had pictured. And her machine had avoided them as if it were—well, afraid was obviously a foolish word to apply to a machine, but it had certainly made off with a speedy discretion, not dropping back to its earlier pace until they were out of sight. Was it one of such things, she wondered, which had so narrowly missed her in the bushes? The sun sank, and a brief twilight quickly gave way to a star-pricked darkness. It was strange to gaze up and see the stars looking again as they had looked from Earth: twinkling points in a bed of darkest blue, no longer flaring sparks in the utter blackness of space. The fading of the daylight seemed to have no effect upon the machine's judgment, for their pace was undiminished. Daylight, darkness or, subsequently, the cold deceptive rays of the Martian moons made no difference to its accuracy. But into Joan's mind that moonlight, flooding across the waste of shining sand and throwing clear-cut purple shadows beneath the rocks, drove still deeper the sense of desolation and decay.

It seemed to her that already they had been travelling for several hours, but there was no sign that this nightmare journey would ever finish; she began to fear that, for her, it would end in the air in her pack giving out. She would die, gasping for breath, and this metal monster would go rushing on across the desert, bearing only her corpse. She had not thought to ask Dale how long the air would last, and every moment became haunted by the fear that she might even now be drawing her last breath. Then, like a sudden message to rouse her out of her despondency, there came the glint of lights some-where ahead. They showed only for a few seconds before the next rise blotted them out, but they gave her new hope. She thanked God that something somewhere on Mars had need of artificial light. . . .

A few more miles of desert fell behind and the machine's feet began to click upon a hard, level surface. A high, black bulk rose in front of them, cutting an increasing patch of darkness in the moonlit sky. The machine held straight on into the shadows. Tall walls reared up on either hand, shutting them into a trench of darkness. The sky overhead was suddenly blotted out. Of the lights she had seen there was now no trace. Not the faintest glimmer broke the pressing blackness. Yet there was a pervading sense of movement all about, of things which were stirring close by in a gloom which her frightened eyes tried in vain to penetrate. From time to time something would brush gently against her in pass-ing and in her ears was a continuous pattering of metal upon stone, but try as she would, she could discern no more than an occasional deeper darkness—as likely as not, a trick of her straining eyes.

Then, at last, she saw the lights again. A turn brought them face to face with a tall building, its façade studded with glowing windows. At ground level a large open doorway poured a fan-shaped beam over the open space in front. By its light she was able to see a number of machines, similar to that which held her, hurrying to and fro. Without a pause she was hurried into a group of several others which was approaching the doorway. Just across the threshold she was set down. A few metal-lic sounds issued from her machine's speaker, then it was gone, scurrying away into the outside darkness. A mo-ment later massive doors slid together, cutting off all hope of escape.

Joan, stiff and giddy from her imprisonment in the constricting tentacles, leaned weakly against the wall while her circulation painfully restored itself. She looked about her with a mixture of curiosity and apprehension. The room was some thirty feet square, bare and cold.

Two sides of it were formed of smoothly dressed, reddish stone, another by the doors through which she had entered, and the fourth, opposite them, by a pair of similar doors. For company she had some half-dozen of the six-legged machines. None of them paid any attention to her, and when after an apparently purposeless interval, the doors on the far side opened, they at once scurried busily away. Joan followed, wonderingly.

Her first impression was of a city of light within the city of darkness—an impression which, she was to find later, fell but little short of the truth. She entered a vast circular hall filled with light from sources which she could not detect. The high roof was slightly domed and must, she thought, have been fully three hundred feet above her at its centre. The width of the place was fully twice its height. Broad balconies, interconnected in some places by staircases and in others by slopes, circled the walls at even intervals. From them arched openings led back into unseen passages or rooms. Round the ground-floor level a series of similar though larger arches was spaced, and between them in constant streams moved machines seeming perpetually in a hurry. She watched them a while as they passed, some burdened, others with their tentacles coiled in rest, but all moving at a constant speed upon their unguessable errands. The only sounds were the scuttering shuffle of their feet and the aggregate purring of the instruments within the casings. She watched them with a kind of absent wonder, at a loss to know what she should do next. The object which had driven her on to the *Gloria Mundi* had been accomplished. Now that she was free of the tentacles her fear of the machines had subsided, but she felt stranded and forlorn. She wondered why they had brought her here, but because they were machines they were alien, and their motives were likely to be un-understandable. She was tempted to accost one and make it understand what she wanted. But what did she want? Not, certainly, to be carried back across those miles of desert with an ever-increasing fear of her air giving out. . . .

Then, abruptly, her decision was taken out of her

hands. A touch on her arm caused her to turn, and she found herself face to face, not with a machine, but with a man.

For several seconds she stared at him without moving. So far from wearing protective clothing, he was clad only in a pair of kilted shorts made from some gleaming material and fastened about his waist by a worked metal belt. His skin was of a reddish tinge, his chest broad and deep, and he was but little taller than herself. His head, beneath its covering of black hair, was of quite unusual size, and the ears, though they were not unsightly and grew closely, were decidedly bigger than those of any Earthman. The rest of his features were unusual only for the fineness of their formation without suggesting weakness and their regularity without loss of character. The eyes were dark and yet penetrating. They seemed to suggest a faint long melancholy, yet they were not truly sad. A queer creature, she thought, but with a kind of charm ... Then, as she watched, there came a slight crinkling at the corners of the eyes and a friendly smile about his mouth. She never again thought of him as a 'queer creature'....

He lifted one hand and signed that she should take off the oxygen mask, but she hesitated. It might be safe enough for him, but her lung capacity could scarcely compare with that beneath his great chest. He repeated the sign insistently, pointing back towards the doors through which she had come. It occurred to her for the first time that the purpose of the double doors must have been that of an airlock. She lifted her mask experimentally. It seemed all right; moreover, as she breathed without its assistance she realized that the air was not only denser within the building, but warmed. She slipped the mask right off with a sigh of relief. It became the man's turn to stare, and hers to return the friendly smile. He spoke. She guessed that he was using the same language as the machines, but his voice was full and pleasing. She shook her head, still smiling, but it was clear that the gesture was as unfamiliar to him as his words were to her. She ripped open the fastener of her suit impatiently and felt in her pockets. No pencil nor pen, but among other femininities almost unused during the voyage she found a lipstick: that would have to serve. She crouched down and explained her difficulty in carmine characters on the floor. The man understood: he took the lipstick from her and wrote an instruction for her to follow him.

CHAPTER XVIII

NEWCOMERS

THE sun sank lower and the shadows stretched long distorted fingers across the desert as though the powers of darkness were reaching out to grasp the land. Desert and sky were repainted by the reddened glow, and even the bushes to the west lost for a few short minutes their dreary reality and underwent a fiery glorification. Presently the last arc sank below their tops; a few fugitive red gleams escaped between the swaying branches, and then night came. Through their padded suits the men from the *Gloria Mundi* felt something of the chill which crept across the Martian sands.

Four times the rank of machines had made a suicidal advance, and four times it had retreated to re-equip itself with parts of the fallen. Now it stood inactive, but ominous; a line of grotesque shapes in dim silhouette against the darkening sky.

The situation was telling on the four men. The very inhumanity of their enemies, their uncanniness and, above all, their unknown potentialities made it impossible for them to maintain the front they might have shown to normal dangers. Their minds seemed to alternate between contempt for mere undirected mechanism, and an exaggerated fear of it. The predicament was getting on their nerves.

'Damn the things,' muttered the doctor. 'I believe they *know* we're caught. They're only machines. They don't need food and drink, and if they need air at all, they've got enough. Standing there like that, using no fuel—whatever their fuel may be—they're good for a century if they like. We've got to move sooner or later—and, damn them, they *know* we've got to move.'

'No good getting the wind up,' Dale advised curtly. 'We can last a good many hours yet. Something may happen before then.'

Froud agreed. 'A planet capable of producing things like that is capable of making anything happen. How long is the night in these parts?'

'Not much longer than at home. We're pretty near the equator.'

The first moon, Deimos, slid up from the ragged horizon, and the sand turned silver beneath it. The polished hull of the ship glittered under it, seeming tantalizingly close, but the rank of machines also gleamed, drawn across the way. The moonlight seemed to invest the metal shapes with a harsher relentlessness, and the sharp shadows it cast from them were even more uncouth than the originals. The men lay silent, each racking his brains for a plan. Nearly two hours passed, and the night became brighter still.

'Lord, isn't that glorious?' Froud said.

The second moon, the smaller Phobos, raced up the sky, rushing to overtake Deimos. They looked up at it.

'What a speed! You can see it go.'

Dugan was the least impressed.

'You'd show speed, too, if you had to do the round trip in seven and a half hours,' he said practically.

Dale rose suddenly to his feet.

'I've had enough of this. I'm going to make a break for it. You can cover me. Those machines must have packed up for the night. They've not moved since before sunset.'

But he was wrong. He had gone less than a dozen yards before the rank stirred, clanking faintly in the thin air. He hesitated and advanced a further couple of paces.

'Come back,' Dugan called. 'You'll never be able to rush it at that distance.'

Dale recognized the truth of it. Even with the increased speed and agility which Mars gave he would not stand a chance of escaping all the tentacles which would grope for him. He turned reluctantly and came slowly back.

Phobos overtook its fellow moon and disappeared. Before long Deimos had followed it round to the other side of the world. In the succeeding dimness the machines were scarcely distinguishable. The four men depended on their ears to give them the first warning of movement, but there was nothing to hear save the faint singing of the wind-stirred sand. They began to suffer from hunger and thirst—particularly thirst. The small quantities of water in their bottles had long ago given out, and their only food, hard cakes of chocolate, had increased their desire for drink. More than an hour passed without anyone speaking.

'There's only one thing for it,' Dale said at last. 'We shall have to do the attacking. If our ammunition holds out we may have a chance, if it doesn't, well, it can't be as bad as what will happen if we stay here. The orders will be: "Shoot for their lenses, and keep clear of their tentacles." '

In his own mind he had not much doubt that he was suggesting the impossible, but with a choice between a quick end and lingering asphyxiation he preferred the former both for himself and for his men.

'You, Dugan and Froud, take the sides——'

'Wait a minute! What's that?' The doctor held his head a little on one side, listening. The others caught the sound. A deep throbbing, growing momentarily louder. They placed it somewhere beyond the canal. Evidently the diaphragms of the machines had picked it up too. The line could be seen faintly stirring.

Low in the western sky a gleam of red light became visible. The throbbing grew quickly to a thunderous roar. Dugan was the first to see the effect on the machines. He looked down in time to see them scampering for the cover of the bushes.

'Now's our chance,' he cried, and with the others behind him he ran down that side of the sandhill which was closest to the *Gloria Mundi*.

The noise from the sky became a crashing, deafening din. Whatever was up there seemed to be making straight for them. Dale and Froud flung themselves flat on the sand with their hands clamped over their ears, and a moment later the other two did the same. The whole world seemed to be cracking and trembling with a noise which split the very sky asunder. Louder and yet louder until noise could be no louder. A sheet of flame like a long fiery banner trailed across the sky bathed the desert with a queer, unnatural light. There was a tremor of the ground. Abruptly the noise stopped, leaving behind it a shocking silence. A scorching breath as hot as a flame itself swept over the sand. A rush of cooler air followed, raising a miniature sandstorm. Froud rolled over on his side, blinking at Dale through the dust. Dale was temporarily deaf from the uproar, and though he saw Froud's mouth moving, he could hear nothing. But he guessed the question.

'That,' he bawled back, 'was another rocket.'

Dale looked out of the window. The other rocket lay perhaps two miles away, her after part just visible above the curve of a sandhill.

'But where the devil can she have come from?' he asked at large for approximately the tenth time.

The four of them were safely back in the living-room. The *Gloria Mundi* was intact. The machines they had seen moving about her had either been unable to open her or uninquisitive enough to be satisfied with an exterior examination. In her crew, curiosity about the new arrival was warring with a desire for sleep. In any case they must wait before finding out more, for the oxygen cylinders needed recharging—a process which would normally have been Burns' job, but which now fell to Dugan.

'Heaven knows,' said Froud. 'Bigger than the *G.M.*, isn't she?'

'Difficult to tell. She may be nearer than she looks. Distance is so damned deceptive here.'

The doctor joined them.

'What next?' he asked. 'Do we look for Joan, or do we investigate the stranger?'

Dale frowned. 'If we had any clue at all, I'd say look for her, but as it is, what can we do? We've not the slightest idea what happened to her, we daren't split up to search, in fact we can't even risk searching all four of us together. Honestly, I don't think there's much hope.'

'I see.' The doctor nodded slowly. 'You think she's gone the way Burns went?'

'Something like that, I'm afraid.'

They all stared out over the inhospitable desert, avoiding one another's eyes.

'A very brave lady. I'm glad she was right,' said the doctor.

There was a long pause before Froud said, with unwonted diffidence:

'May I suggest that rather than investigate the stranger, as Doc puts it, we let the stranger investigate us? To tell you the truth, I'm beginning to feel that this place is far less healthy than we supose; certainly it's not as empty as we thought, and it seems to me that if anyone is to be caught in the open either by the machines returning or by anything else that may show up, it would be better if it were the other fellows.'

Dale hesitated. He was actively anxious to find out more about the other rocket, yet Froud had made a point.

'You think the machines will come back?'

'If the arrival of one rocket interested them, the arrival of two should interest them still more,' Froud fancied. The doctor supported him:

'I don't see that we are justified in exposing ourselves to unnecessary risks. After all, our trip here will have been of no use to anyone if we don't make the trip back again.'

'And you, Dugan?' Dale asked.

Dugan looked round, his hand still on the valve of the oxygen chargers.

'I don't care. But I do know one thing: I want to get

back to Earth. And I want to tell all those people who laughed at Joan and her father that they were right. Just now it all rather depends, doesn't it, on whether we've any chance of getting back at all?'

'Meaning?'

'Well, we hadn't a large margin of spare fuel to begin with, and Joan's extra weight made us use more than we had reckoned. Have we enough to take us back, and to stop when we get there?'

All three looked at Dale. He answered slowly:

'I think we have—anyway, we've more than a sporting chance of making it. You see, whereas six of us came here, it seems that only four will return. Besides, there are quite a number of heavy things such as rifles and ammunition which we can jettison. They'll be of no further use to us after we leave here.'

Dugan nodded. 'I hadn't thought of that. Well, then, I'm with Froud and Doc. Let the other rocket people come and look at us if they want to.'

Several hours later Dale still sat by the window, keeping watch. Occasionally he looked across at one of the others, half enviously. He wished that he too could have lain down to catch up some overdue sleep, but he knew that it would be useless for him to attempt it while the problem of the other ship's identity remained unsolved. It was possible that the ship was native to Mars, but he did not find it easy to swallow such a palatable hope. She was meant for space travel—no doubt about that. Otherwise she would have had wings, big wings, too, in this thin air. Was she, he wondered, a Martian space ship returning home from another planet, possibly from Earth? Joan's story seemed to show that this world had sent out at least one messenger successfully. Again he was anxious to think so, but all the time something at the back of his mind was repeating insistently the thing he least wanted to believe: that this ship had followed the *Gloria Mundi* from Earth.

That was the fear which would not let him rest.

He had been the first to reach Mars, but that was a job only half done. He must be the first to tell Earth about

Mars. The leader of the first successful inter-planetary journey in the history of the world. Dale Curtance, the Conqueror of Space—a name which should never be forgotten. And now he faced the possibility of a rival who might snatch immortality out of his very hands.

Had he been able, he would have taken off this very moment, heading the *Gloria Mundi* for Earth with all the speed of which she was capable, but it was impracticable for several reasons, of which the most immediate was that she now lay on her side. Before they could start, they would have to raise her to the perpendicular.

Dale was not a good loser. He had won too often since that day when he had led the first equatorial dash round the world. The Martian venture was to be the crown of his career. Not for the five million dollars—to hell with that, he had spent more than that on building and fueling the *G.M.* No, it was for the triumph of being not just the first, but for a time the only man to have linked the planets. It was the thought that this other ship might mean his failure in that which kept him at the window for almost unendurable hours while his companions slept and daylight came again.

Again he asked himself who could have sent her. The Keuntz people? Had he been misinformed about them after all? Yet who else in the world could have built a ship capable of it?

Then, on the crest of a rise in the direction of the other ship appeared a few black dots. Machines or men? He found the spare pair of glasses and focused them. Then he crossed hurriedly to the sleepers and shook them.

'Wake up, there!'

'Damn you,' murmured Froud. 'Machines back?'

'No, men from the other ship. Coming this way.'

CHAPTER XIX

VAYGAN

THEY stopped in a room which led by a short passage off the third balcony level. The man signed to Joan to remain, and she seated herself on a box-like stool with a padded top while he disappeared through another door-way.

As she waited she examined the place by the light which diffused evenly from the entire ceiling. It was a bare, severely simple room. The furnishings consisted of several similar padded stools, one larger cube, presumably for use as a table, and a low, broad seat which might be either couch or bed, set against one of the walls. The side opposite the entrance was completely taken up by a single window through which she could see the great bulks of black buildings silhouetted against the moonlit sky and, between them, a glimpse of the desert stretching coldly away to infinity.

The floor and the solid walls were coloured a pale green. On the left was the opening through which her guide had gone, to either side of it were set rectangular panels of a smoky-grey, glass-like substance suggesting more purpose than mere decoration. Here and there in the other walls narrow slits outlined the doors of cupboards or removable panels set flush. To the right, close to the end of the divan-like seat, she noticed a control board with a great show of levers and knobs.

It seemed a bleak place, with something of an institutional air: not unfriendly, but impersonal. It needed furnishing with books, a picture or two and flowers. Then she laughed at herself—disapproving of a room here because it was not like a room at home! Books and pictures here—and flowers. With a sudden sadness she wondered how many long ages had passed since this weary old planet had grown its last flower. . . . This room was too hard, too purely utilitarian. Better suited for housing a machine than a human being; one could not feel that it was lived in—yet her guide was human enough. . . .

The warmth of her padded overall became oppressive in the heated building, and the man returned to find her in the process of disentangling herself from it. He placed the two bowls of liquid which he was carrying upon the larger cube and approached with curiosity. Her leather suit seemed to puzzle him; he fingered it, feeling its texture, but could make nothing of it. She thought that he watched her with a faint amusement as she ran a comb through her hair.

Momentous occasions so seldom come up to expectations, she told herself. This was a turning-point in history: the people of two planets were meeting for the first time—and she was behaving as if she had dropped in to pay a call. It was an occasion which called for one of those undying remarks with which historical characters have greeted the successive crises of the race. Instead, she was combing her hair. . . . Oh, well, there was no audience here; she could think up the immortal phrase later on—probably most of the historical characters had done the same. She smiled again at the Martian and took the bowl he was offering.

The colourless liquid in it was not water. It had a faint, indeterminable flavour and a greater consistency. Whatever it was, its tonic properties were immense; new strength and a feeling of well being seemed to pour into her. The man nodded as if satisfied with the effect. He opened one of the panels in the right-hand wall and withdrew two trays of wax-like substance. He scratched the surface of one with a series of characters and handed it to her. The other he kept himself. Joan prepared to give her whole mind to her first lesson in spoken Martian.

The method of instruction appeared at first to be simple. He would write a word with which she was already familiar, saying it aloud at the same time, while she then attempted to repeat it after him. She had expected that the process of turning her written vocabulary into vocal would present no great difficulties. She saw herself able in a very short time to rattle off the words she held in her mind's eye. But her disillusionment was rapid. She found herself quite unable to grasp the principles of its expression. To begin with she had it settled in her own mind that the characters were of the nature of phonetic signs—that a certain sign, for instance could be said to represent 't'. But she found that though it might represent 't' for the first two or three times she met it, it was just as likely to turn up in a word with no 't' value at all. As in English 'c' may be either 'k' or 's', and 's' may be either 'c' or 'z', so, but with much more bewildering variation, were the Martian characters capable of changing their values. Finer gradations in vowel sounds almost eluded her ear even after constant repetition, but worse still was the discovery of a number of consonants in the form of unfamiliar clicking sounds which utterly defeated her best efforts at imitation. It was no good that her teacher should sit opposite her, mouthing exaggeratedly in encouragement; they were tricks his tongue had learned in early youth, her own refused to perform them.

She felt a growing sense of desperation. It was ridiculous that she should have worked so hard upon the script only to be baffled by this business of turning it into sound. She had an exasperating feeling that there was a principle somewhere that she had missed; a principle which once grasped would make the whole thing as clear as daylight. But if there was it continued to elude her. The longer the lesson went on, the deeper she got bogged in misunderstanding and the wilder grew her guesses at the sounds of the words she wrote.

At the end of two hours she faced her teacher with tears in her eyes. She could identify certain things in the room, the stools, the window, the bowls on the table, and that was almost the limit of her progress. She was both miserable and exasperated. There was so much she wanted to ask about himself, his city and the machines. To write all that would be slow and tedious, moreover, she had quickly discovered the limitations of her own vocabulary. She smoothed over her wax tray and wrote:

'I can't understand. It is too difficult,' with a sense that their minds were working by different rules, each incapable of grasping the difficulties which beset the other. Something the same situation might have occurred, she felt, if Alice had tried to teach French to the Mad Hatter. It appeared too, that the stimulating effect of the drink was wearing off, for she again felt tired and sleepy.

The man took the tray from her and read the message. He looked at her intently again, seeming to examine her from a new angle. After a pause he wrote beneath her own words:

'I could, if you like, try——'

She could not understand the final word: it was new to her, but she agreed almost without hesitation. Disgusted with her own failure to learn, but still more desperately anxious to know his language, she scarcely cared what means he took to achieve it as long as they were successful. His own expression was not entirely confident.

'With us it would be certain,' he wrote, 'but your mind may be different. I will try.'

She allowed him to lead her across to the divan and lay down there as he directed. He drew one of the stools close beside it and sat down, holding her gaze unwaveringly with his own. His eyes seemed to lose all expression. They no longer looked at hers, but through them as though they were exploring the mind behind: compelling and examining with utter impersonality her most secret thoughts. A moment of panic seized her as her feelings revolted against the invasion of her privacy, and she tried to shake his visual hold, but his eyes broke down her resistance, forbidding her even to close her lids. The room began to whirl, becoming unreal and distorted as though it were slipping away. Not only the room, but herself and everything about her was slipping away. Only the eyes in a blurred face remained steady. Her own clung to them as to the only fixtures in a reeling universe.

It was as though she were waking from sleep, yet with a sense of exhaustion. The eyes were still fixed on her own, but as she watched they lost intensity as if they withdrew from her into themselves. The face about them became clear and then the room beyond. Her sense of time had gone awry: it seemed both long ago and yet only a few minutes since she had lain down, but she could see that outside there was complete darkness and both the moons had set. She turned her head back to face the man on the stool once more.

'I'm so tired,' she said. 'I want to sleep.'

'You shall,' he said. He carefully rearranged the rug which she had not known was covering her.

Not until he had gone from the room did she realize that he had understood her, and she, him.

At her second waking he was beside her again, offering her a bowl of the same colourless liquid that she had drunk the night before. The sun was shining into the room from the clear, purplish sky. She did not speak until she had handed the empty bowl back to him.

'Your name is Vaygan?' she asked, but before he could answer she added: 'Of course it is. I *know* it is, but I don't understand how I know it. It's strange—I'm speaking your language now, but I feel as if it were my own. I don't have to think about it. You hypnotized me?'

'Something like that,' he agreed,' 'but more complex. I put you into a trance and taught you. It is difficult to explain simply. One can in certain circumstances and for certain purposes alter the mind. No, "alter" is the wrong word. It is more as if one inserted a new section of knowledge in the mind. Tell me, how do you feel now?'

'Rather bewildered,' Joan smiled.

'Of course. But no more than puzzled?'

'No.' A sudden misgiving took her. 'You haven't—done anything to my mind. Not done anything which will make me not me—I mean, make me think differently?'

'I hope not, in fact, I think not. I was most careful. It was very difficult. Your mind seems less clear than ours. There are overlaps between unconnected subjects and impediments to a proper balance of judgment so that it works differently. Its logical processes are slow, its illogical conclusions very frequent, but also slow. I took a long time: it would have been no good to either of us if I had spoilt it.'

'I don't think I quite understand that.'

'Shall I say that your mind has more vitality but poorer control than ours?'

'All right, we'll let it go at that for the moment. As long as I'm sure that I'm still me, I don't mind.'

And, surprisingly, she found that she did not mind. She did not in the least resent his violation of her most secret thoughts now that it was an accomplished fact, though she knew that she would have shrunk from the prospect had she fully understood his intentions the previous night. Subsequently she wondered more than once whether he had not seen the likelihood of resentment and taken means to prevent it. For the present her delight at the annihilation of the language obstacle easily swept away other considerations.

She demanded to know more of the machines, of life on Mars, of himself and his people. The questions poured out in a string, making him smile.

'You are so eager,' he said, as if in apology. 'So anxious to learn. We must have been like that once—long ago.'

'Long ago?'

'I meant when our race was young. We are old now: our planet is old: we are born old compared with the oldest of you. Had you come just a few centuries later, you might have found no men; our long history would have ended. You ask of life on Mars. I scarcely know how to answer you for life, to you, is a thing of promise, whereas for us—but I shall show you. This city you are in was called—is called Hanno. It is the biggest of the seven cities which are still inhabited, yet there are no more than three thousand men and women in it now. Fewer and fewer children are born to us. Perhaps that is well. Each generation only prolongs our decay. We have had a glorious past—but a glorious past is bitterness for a child with a hopeless future. For you who think of life as striving, it will be difficult to understand.'

'But can you do nothing?' Joan asked. 'You must know so much. Can't you find out why less children are born, and cure it?'

'We could, perhaps, but is it worth it? Would you wish to bear a child for a life of imprisonment—able to live only in our artificial conditions such as this? We have tried all we can. We have even created monsters; scarcely human creatures which were able to live in the thin air. But it needs more than mere physical strength to survive on a planet such as this where nothing useful as food can grow. Our monsters were too unintelligent to survive—we ourselves, too, unadapted physically. Life as you see it means very little to us now. Quite soon we shall be gone and there will be only the machines.'

'The Machines?' Joan repeated. 'What are the Machines? They are the puzzle which brought me here.' She told him of the machine which had somehow reached Earth. 'I felt nervous of it,' she owned, 'and I felt nervous of your machines last night. I think that is the first reaction of all of us to our own machines. Some never get beyond it, others get used to it, but when we think of machines we feel that in spite of all they have given us and all they do for us there is something malignant about them. Their very presence forces us down ways we do not want to go. We have felt that since we first had them; there have been books, plays, pictures with the malevolence of the Machine for their theme. The idea persists of the eventual conquest of man by the Machine. You don't seem to see them like that.'

'We don't. But I told you that our minds work differently in many ways. Our first, simple machines were designed to help us over difficulties, and they were successful.'

'But so were ours, weren't they?'

'Well, were they? I learned quite a lot of your history when I looked into your mind last night, and it seemed to me that they were not. Machines have come early into your race history. They were not necessary. They were thrust suddenly upon a race with no great problems, a race, moreover, so primitive that it was still—is still—full of superstition. We did not invent the machine until it was necessary for our survival. You invented the machine and caused it to be necessary for your survival. It saved us, but you thrust it upon a world not yet ready for it, and you have failed to adapt to it.'

'But we have changed. We've changed enormously. Our whole outlook is utterly different from that of our great-grandfathers and even of our grandfathers. We recognize that in the modern world one must move with the times.'

'You have changed, perhaps, but very little—and that under continual protest. In you, and I take it that you are typical of your race, the sentimental resistance to change is immense.' He paused, looking at her with a slight frown. 'On Mars,' he continued, 'man has been the most adaptable of all the animal creations.'

'And on Earth,' she put in.

'I wonder? It seems to me that your race may be in grave danger—almost as if you may be losing the power to adapt. Man's rise and his survival depend on his adaptability. It was because the old masters of the world could not adapt that they lost their mastery. New conditions defeated them. You have created new conditions, but you have scarcely disturbed your ways of living to suit them. It is little wonder to me that you fear the Machine. Even while you use it you try to live the lives of craftsmen. You resent the change because you know subconsciously, and will not admit openly, that it means an utter break with the past. A new force has come into your world which makes an end inevitable. Which is it to be—an end of your system of life; or of your system and yourselves together?'

Joan looked puzzled. 'But do you mean that all tradition is to be thrown aside? Why, you talked just now of your own glorious past.'

'Tradition is a useful weed for binding the soil, but it grows too thickly and chokes the rest. Periodically it must be burned out. Consider where you would be now if the traditions of your ancient races had not been destroyed from time to time.'

She was silent a while, looking back at the practices of earlier civilizations. Human sacrifice, enslavement, cannibalism, religious prostitution, trial by ordeal, exposure of girl children and plenty more of them, all honourable customs at some age. Most of them had been burnt out, as Vaygan put it, in the west, at any rate. Others were due to be dropped: war, execution, gold fetishism...

'It is not sensible to use only one eye when one has the power to focus with two,' Vaygan said. 'The problems you have raised will have to be examined with your whole intelligence, they cannot be left to solve themselves.'

'Did your people face them once?' she asked.

'With us it was different. Our machines put order into a disorganized world. Yours have done the opposite.'

'I think I see. But what are these queer machines of yours? They're nothing like ours. They seem to think for themselves.'

'Why should they not?'

'I don't know, except that it seems fantastic to me. It was the theme of those tales I told you about and I find it rather frightening. Do your machines rule you, or do you rule them?'

Vaygan was first puzzled and then amused.

'You are determined to assume an antagonism between machines and men. You don't understand them. It's your persistent mishandling of them that makes you afraid of them. Why should there be antagonism? There was a time when we could not exist without them nor they without us, and now, though that no longer holds, the collaboration continues. Doubtless if they wished they could make an end of us today, but why should they? We are doomed inevitably: they will go on.'

'You mean that they will survive you?' Joan asked incredulously.

'Certainly they will survive. I think that if you were to dig down deeply into our real motives you would find that the chief reason why we have not committed suicide or died out already from discouragement at the futility of existence is our faith in the machines. For many thousands of years we have fought Nature and held our own, but at last she has the upper hand. She is sweeping us away as she has swept the rest on to her huge rubbish heap where the bones of the dinosaurs moulder on the fossils of a million ages. What has been the good of us? Nothing, it seems, and yet ... our minds will not accept that. There lingers, perhaps illogically, the idea of a purpose behind it all.... But physically we can go on no longer.

'For any other species of animal it would mean utter extinction, but we have what the other animals have never had—mind. That is our last trick. Our minds will not die yet. The machines are as truly the children of our minds as you are the child of your mother's body. They are the next step in evolution, we hand over to them.'

'Evolution! But evolution is a gradual modification. It is impossible to evolve from flesh to metal.'

'You think so? Because hitherto it has been so? But you overlook the factor which never was in evolution until we came—mind, again: the greatest factor of all, and it is producing the greatest mutation of all.'

Joan objected. 'But what is a machine? Why should it go on? It's not alive, it has no soul, it can't love. Why should a collection of metal parts go on?'

'Why should a collection of chemical parts go on? You do not understand our machines. The stuff of life is in them as it is in you. A slightly different form of life, perhaps, but you tend to judge too much by appearances. After all, if a man is equipped with four artificial limbs of metal, if he needs glasses to see with, instruments to hear with and false teeth to eat with, he is still alive. So there is life of a kind in the machines' casings. That their frames are of metal and not of calcium is neither here nor there.

'And as for love ... Does an amoeba love? Do fish love? But they go on—they reproduce. Love is just our particular mechanism for continuation; the fish have another; the machines yet another.'

'A machine with the urge to reproduce!' Joan could not keep the scoffing note out of her voice.

'Why not?'

'But it is metal—not flesh and blood.'

'A tree is wood, but it reproduces. Continuity has a deeper cause than the call of flesh to flesh—if it were not so, our race would long ago have declined the discomforts of breeding. It is the will to power which leads us—love is its very humble servant.'

'And your machines have this will to power?'

'Can you doubt it? Consider the inexorability of machines; add intelligence to that and what can withstand their will?'

Joan shrugged her shoulders. She said, with hesitation:

'I can't really understand. Our machines are so very different. The bare idea of an intelligent machine is difficult for me to grasp.'

'You have discovered the machine so lately—you have no broad idea yet of what you have found.'

'We have got far enough to build a machine which could bring us here——'

She stopped abruptly. For these hours she had completely forgotten her companions of the *Gloria Mundi*. She had last seen them standing disarmed beside the great canal while Burns led her away. She wondered with a rush of remorseful anxiety how they had fared; whether they, too, had fallen victims to the things that moved in the bushes. Turning to Vaygan again she asked not very hopefully if he had news of them. He smiled at her tone.

'Certainly. I will show them to you if you like.'

'Show me?'

He turned a switch on the board beside her. One of the grey panels shone translucently. The scene was blurred, but as he worked the controls it cleared, steadied and focused. One seemed to be looking down on desert, scrub and a part of the canal from a great height. In one corner of the screen there gleamed a small silvery bullet shape. He made another adjustment. With a dizzying effect, as though she were falling towards it, Joan watched the rocket enlarge until it filled the whole screen. She frowned a little; it looked wrong somehow—perhaps an odd effect of perspective? Vaygan manipulated his instrument to give a view as of one walking slowly round the ship. Joan grew more puzzled, but not until they had, in effect, rounded the nose did she speak.

'But that's not the *Gloria Mundi*,' she said. 'It's got queer letters on it; I can't read them. I don't understand what's happened.'

Vaygan looked incredulous.

'But—wait a minute.' He pressed another switch. A metallic voice came from another speaker. Vaygan asked a question and listened attentively to the reply. He turned back to Joan.

'They say another rocket landed two hours before dawn.'

'Then this must be it, but where is ours?'

He altered the switches. Again the panel appeared as a window through which they saw a scene from far above. The country seemed to move slowly beneath them as on a panorama. A second silver shell came into view.

'There she is,' Joan said quickly.

Again there came that uncanny sense of falling. This time there was no doubt. She could read *Gloria Mundi* in large letters just abaft the cabin windows. Through the fused quartz of the window she was even able to make out Dale's features. He was staring intently at something beyond their field of view. Before she could suggest it, Vaygan had altered the controls to show a party of men crossing the sand with that odd, high-stepping action which the low gravity induced. She noticed that they wore oxygen masks of an unfamiliar pattern and that they carried rifles.

'The men from the other rocket,' she said.

'Your friends don't seem pleased to see them,' he remarked.

Again the screen altered. The familiar living-room of the *Gloria Mundi* appeared so that Joan was almost able to believe herself seated in it. She could see Dale's back as he stood staring out of the window. The doctor was rubbing his eyes and yawning. Dugan had taken a pistol from a locker and was loading a clip with cartridges. Froud had set up a movie-camera beside Dale at the window. He was attempting to prevent all three legs of the tripod from slipping on the metal floor and to work the instrument at the same time.

'We will listen to them, and you shall tell me what they are saying,' Vaygan suggested. He pressed over another small switch.

An eruption of outrageous profanity in Froud's voice tore through the room.

Vaygan looked startled.

'What was that?' he asked.

Joan laughed.

'Quite untranslatable, I'm afraid. Poor dear! How I must have cramped his style all these weeks.'

CHAPTER XX

KARAMINOFF MAKES PROPOSALS

'—AND may the blasted thing blister in hell,' Froud hoped fervently. He looked round wildly for inspiration and caught sight of the doctor.

'Here, Doc, drop the exercises and for Heaven's sake come and hold this thundering contraption while I work it. Must get a shot of these chaps, whoever they are.'

The doctor ambled across amiably and laid hold of the tripod. Froud busied himself with focus and aperture awhile. Dugan slipped the loaded pistol into his pocket and joined them.

'Who the dickens do you think they are?' he asked. The question was directed at Dale, but it was Froud who answered.

'Well, there's one thing they're not, and that's Martians. See the way they keep on nearly falling over themselves? Wonder if we looked as damn silly at first?' he said, as he set the camera going.

The approaching party stopped a hundred yards away and appeared to consult. Of the six men, the tallest was obviously the leader. They watched him raise his arm and point to the Union Jack which Dale had set up. He made some remark which amused the rest. Dale frowned as he watched, not so much at their actions as at his inability to identify the leader. He had no longer any doubt that this second rocket also came from Earth, and the number of men capable of making the flight was limited. It was practically impossible that he should not have met or at least known the man by hearsay. But the oxygen masks worn by all six were fitted with goggles and completely obscured the faces save for chins and mouths.

The party resumed its clumsy advance, making for the window. In the *Gloria Mundi*'s living-room there was silence save for the clicking of the camera. Froud broke it.

'This ought to make a good picture: "March of the Bogey Men of Mars," ' he said.

A few paces away the newcomers halted again. One could catch the gleam of eyes behind the glasses, but it was still impossible to identify the features. The leader was looking at Dale. He was making signs, pointing first to himself and then to the *Gloria Mundi*. Dale hesitated, then he held up three fingers and nodded, indicating the position of the entrance. He turned to Dugan.

'See to the airlock, but don't let more than three of them in, to begin with.'

Dugan crossed the room and pulled over the lever opening the outer door. The glow of a small bulb told him that someone had stepped into the lock. He pressed back the lever, spun the wheel of a stopcock and watched the pointer of the pressure dial slide back from the neighbourhood of seven towards the normal fifteen pounds. Froud swivelled his camera round and reset it.

'This,' he remarked to the unresponsive Dale, 'is where you step forward with a bright smile and say: "Doctor Livingstone, I presume."'

The inner door of the lock swung open and the tall man entered, stooping a little to avoid striking his head. Inside the room he straightened up and then raised his hand to slip the mask from a long, tanned face. His black, deep sunk eyes watched Dale keenly as he nodded a greeting.

'How do you do, Mr. Curtance?' he said. He spoke in good enough English, but it lacked tonal variation. He turned to the journalist.

'Hullo, Froud.'

Froud's mouth opened, he blinked slightly and quickly recovered himself.

'Well! Well! Well!' he remarked.

'You might introduce me,' the man suggested.

'Of course. Gentlemen, may I present Comrade Karaminoff, he is Commissar of——' He broke off. 'What are you Commissar of just now?' he inquired.

The tall man shrugged. 'Suppose you say Commissar without portfolio at present. One hopes in time to be Commissar for Inter-planetary Affairs.'

'Oh,' said Froud mildly. 'Your hopes were never modest, were they, Karaminoff? Do you remember the time I met you at Gorki? If I remember rightly you were hoping then to be Commissar for the North American Continent.'

'I know. We were misled. The country is still too bourgeois—but it is improving. Quite soon now it will become a Soviet.'

Dale stepped forward. He spoke brusquely:

'Are we to understand that you are the commander of a ship sent here by the Russian Government?'

'That is so, Mr. Curtance. The *Tovaritch* of the U.S.S.R.'

'The *Tovaritch*! But the rumours of her existence were expressly denied by your government.'

157

'Yes, it seemed politic to us—after all, it was our own affair. The Americans kept quiet about theirs, too.'

The entire personnel of the *Gloria Mundi* gaped at him stupidly.

'The Americans! Good God! You don't mean to say that they've got one, too?'

'But certainly. The Keuntz people. Your information does not seem to have been very full, Mr. Curtance.'

'But——' Words failed Dale. He stood dumbfounded, staring at the Russian.

'It would seem to be raining rockets. Most disappointing,' said Froud. 'Tell us, Karaminoff, how many more?'

The other shook his head.

'No more. There was an—er—accident to the German one. Possibly you read about it: it was reported as an explosion in a munitions factory. It would probably have been the best of the lot. The Germans are very clever, you know, and very anxious for colonies.'

'And so there was an—er—accident, was there? H'm, Dale only just frustrated an—er—accident to the *Gloria Mundi*. Very interesting.'

There was a pause during which Karaminoff introduced the other two Russians whom Dugan had admitted. He added:

'And now, I think, it is necessary for us to have some discussion.'

'Just a minute,' Froud put in. 'I'm a bit puzzled by several things. Did you start after or before us?'

'A day or so later.'

'And with millions of square miles of planet to choose from you had the luck to land next door to us?'

'Oh, no, not luck.' The Russian shook his head emphatically. 'We followed you with telescopes. We saw the flames of your rockets as you landed and we marked the spot. Then we held off a little.'

'You *what*?' Dugan burst in.

'We held off.'

Dugan stared first at him and then at Dale. Both of them knew that the *Gloria Mundi* could never have performed such a manoeuvre. An involuntary tinge of respect came into Dugan's voice as he said:

'Your *Tovaritch* must be a wonderful ship.'

'She is,' Karaminoff told him with complacence.

There was a pause. Karaminoff crossed to the western window and looked out thoughtfully. The dreary bushes were waving their papery leaves, the breeze raised occasional scurries of reddish dust, but his eyes were not on these things. He was watching an entirely terrestrial phenomenon—the Union Jack fluttering from its pole.

'I see that you have what you call—staked a claim,' he said, turning to face Dale.

'By the authority of Her Majesty I have annexed this territory to the British Commonwealth of Nations,' Dale told him, not without slight pomposity.

'Dear me! The entire planet? I suppose so. There is nothing modest about the English in matters of territory.'

'You'd have done the same if you had got here first,' Dugan put in impatiently. 'But you've been unlucky, that's all.'

Karaminoff smiled. He said conversationally:

'The English man of action amazes me. He has the unique gift of living simultaneously in the twentieth and seventeenth centuries. Technically he is advanced, socially—or should I say anti-socially?—he has stagnated for three hundred years. It needs no straining for my imagination to see an ancestor Curtance planting a flag on a Pacific island in sixteen something and saluting it with the same words as the modern Mr. Curtance must have used here—only, of course, with the word 'Empire" instead of "Commonwealth".'

'Well, why not? It's a fine tradition,' Dugan said with uncertain resentment of the other's tone. 'It made the finest Empire in the world.'

'I agree. But the Romans once had the finest Empire in the world, so did the Greeks, and the Assyrians, they are historical; so is the building of the British Empire. Can't you see that this cool annexation of property is outdated. Your method is a quaint anachronism. Do you really think that just because you have planted that flag here your sovereign right will be recognized? That the other peoples of Earth will stand by and allow you to take this place and do what you like with it? The trouble about you English is that you always think you are playing some kind of game, with the rules conveniently made up by yourselves.'

The doctor spoke for the first time since the Russian's entrance.

'And we are to suppose that you are free from the bourgeois ideal of Imperialism?'

'I am not here to annex or conquer, if that is what you mean.'

'Then just what are you here for?'

'I am here to prevent conquest; to offer to the citizens of Mars union with the Soviet Socialist Republics in a defensive alliance against the greed of capitalist nations which——' He broke off abruptly to glare at the journalist. 'You find something amusing?' he inquired coldly.

Froud stifled his laughter and wiped his eyes.

'So will you when you see the "citizens",' he said with difficulty. 'I'm longing to hear you teach one of our friends of last night to sing the "Internationale". But don't mind me. Go on.'

The doctor put in: 'I suppose I'm pretty dense, but the difference between our missions seems to be chiefly in terms. It boils down to their choosing an alliance with the Empire, or an alliance with the Soviets.'

'If you cannot see the difference between union with us and submission to rule by imperialist and capitalist interests, you must, as you say, be pretty dense.'

The doctor thought for a while.

'All right, we'll take it that I'm dense. Now, what do you propose to do about it?'

Dale broke in before Karaminoff could answer:

'I don't see that we need to prolong this useless discussion any longer. The facts are quite obvious. I have laid first claim here. The other nations, except the Soviets, will naturally honour it.'

The Russian studied him thoughtfully.

'That's just the kind of statement which gets the English a reputation for subtlety. Nobody else can ever believe that such ingenuousness is real. "If the Englishman is as guileless as that, how does he continue to exist?" they ask. One has to confess that it is a mystery and accept it as one accepts other freaks of nature, for I know that you sincerely believe what you say.'

'You think that other nations will dare to dispute our claim? They've no grounds for it whatever.'

'But, my dear man, what need have they of grounds? Who made the rules of this game? Surely the fact that they want territory here is grounds enough. Really, you know, one of the most disheartening sights for persons of vision and acumen during the last few centuries must have been the spectacle of the English blundering about all over the globe and bringing off *coup* after *coup* by combinations of accident and sheer simple faith. It is a wonder that the conception of a planned, intelligent civilization can still exist in the face of it.

'And now, just because you arrived here a few hours ahead of us, you quite honestly think yourselves entitled to all the mineral wealth which this planet may contain.'

'So we are,' Dale and Dugan said, almost together.

Karaminoff turned to look at his two companions.

'Did I not tell you how it would be?' he said, with a smile and a shrug.

One of them answered him rapidly in Russian. Karaminoff said:

'Comrade Vassiloff is bored. He wishes us to—er—cut the cackle.'

'Comrade Vassiloff is a sensible man,' said the doctor. 'Lead out your horses.'

'I will. It is this. There are to be no territorial claims on this land by any nation, government or groups of persons. In such useful exchanges as can be made between Earth and Mars, no nation shall receive preferential treatment. Such commerce shall be under direct governmental control and not open to exploitation by individuals. Mars shall retain the right of self-government and management of policy both internally and externally. There shall be——'

'And yet,' the doctor put in, 'you intend to invite them into union with the Soviets? That hardly seems compatible.'

'If by their free choice they elect——'

'You damned scoundrel,' Dugan shouted. 'You know perfectly well that that will mean rule from Moscow. So that is what you call giving them freedom! Of all the infernal nerve!'

Karaminoff spread his hands.

'You see,' he said, 'even your hot young patriot is sure that they would prefer to join us.'

'Well they won't have the chance. We claim this territory by right of discovery, and we're damn' well going to have it.'

Froud yawned and crossed to the window. He stared out for a few seconds and then beckoned Karaminoff to his side.

'Don't you think you'd better open negotiations with the "citizens" before you formulate any more of the constitution? See, there's a potential comrade lurking in the bushes over there.'

Karaminoff followed the direction of his finger. He could just make out something which moved among the branches and he saw the shine of sunlight upon metal. At that moment one of the three Russians who had remained outside the *Gloria Mundi* came running to the window. He was pointing excitedly in the same direction. Karaminoff nodded and turned back to the rest.

'Very well, we will go now. I will let you know the outcome of my negotiations, but whatever they are, believe me that this is one time that the English are not going to get away with their land grabbing.'

Nobody answered him. The three Russians put on their oxygen masks and passed one by one out of the airlock. The *Gloria Mundi*'s crew watched them rejoin their companions. There was much excited conversation and frequent indications of the bushes, and the party began to move off in that direction. It paused beside

Dale's post. They saw Karaminoff look up at the flag and then back at the ship. The breathing mask hid his features, but they could guess at the smile beneath it. One of the Russians crouched and then launched himself in what would have been an impossible leap on Earth. His outstretched hand caught the flag and tore it free from the pole as he dropped.

'Damned swine!' Dugan shouted. Before the rest could stop him he was across the room and into the airlock.

Karaminoff was reaching up to tie a red flag with a white hammer and sickle upon it to the bare pole when the man beside him suddenly clutched his arm and spun round. One of the others swivelled, firing from his hip at the entrance port. Karaminoff, apparently unmoved, finished fixing his flag and stepped back, waving a hand to the occupants of the ship, but only Froud was at the window to watch him. Dale and the doctor were at the airlock waiting anxiously till the pressures should equalize. The door swung open to reveal Dugan sitting on the floor. His face was purple, and blood was trickling down his leg.

'Silly young fool,' said the doctor.

'Ricochet off the outer door,' Dugan panted. 'In the leg.'

'Lucky for you it isn't asphyxiation. Let me look at it.'

'Missed the swine, too,' Dugan gasped.

'He couldn't reach very high, so his flag's only flying at half-mast, if that's any consolation to you,' said Froud from the window. 'Karaminoff's splitting the gang. The bloke you pipped is going home with another. He himself and the other three are making for the bushes.' He suddenly left the window and dashed across the room. 'Where's that damned telephoto got to. Here, Dale, help me get this thing rigged up. What a chance! Must get a shot of Karaminoff greeting the animated tinware— That's it, right up to the window.—What'll we call it? Look! Look, there's Comrade Clockwork coming out of the bushes now. Oh, boy!'

A mechanical voice chattering urgently cut across all other sounds. Its speed and harshness made it impossible for Joan to catch the words, but she thought it was saying something about a rocket. Vaygan flipped over a switch and the interior of the *Gloria Mundi* faded from the screen, simultaneously her crew's voices were cut off.

'Where?' Vaygan asked sharply.

The voice gabbled a string of unintelligible directions which started him readjusting his dials and switches. The screen lost its opaqueness once more and took on a uniform purple tinge. Until a whisp of tenuous cloud drifted across Joan did not realize that it was showing the Martian sky. Vaygan was watching it intently, slowly turning his dials. Presently a bright spark slid in from one side, and he gave a grunt. Evidently he had found what he wanted. He manipulated the controls to keep it in the middle of the screen.

'What is it?' Joan asked.

'Another rocket—like yours.'

'Another?' She remembered what the Russian had said about an American rocket.

'Can't you get a closer view of it?' she asked.

'Not yet. It's too far away.'

They watched for a time in silence. Swiftly the spark grew from a mere dot to a flaring mass as the rocket dived lower and closer. The tubes were working furiously to break her long fall, belching out vivid gushes of white-hot fire which was carried back along her sides to die in tattered banners of flame in her wake. Nearer and nearer she came, falling like a meteor wrapped in her own inferno of flame. It seemed impossible that in such a blast the ship herself should not be incandescent. Yet she was not out of control. Perceptibly she was slowing. But Vaygan murmured:

'She's coming in too fast—far too fast.'

He could alter the angle of view now so that they seemed to look down on her as they followed her course. The Martian landscape streamed below her in an approaching blur. For a second she slipped out of the picture. Vaygan spun a control and picked her up again. She was dropping fast. Her rockets were erupting like miniature volcanoes, but still her speed was prodigious. The sandhills below her hurtled past indistinguishably. Joan's fists clenched as she watched, and she found herself holding her breath.

'They can't—they can't land at that speed,' she cried. 'Oh!'

Vaygan put his free hand over hers, he said nothing. She wanted to shut out the sight, but her eyes refused to leave the screen.

The rocket was nearly down now. A few hundred feet only above the desert, still going a thousand miles an hour. Joan gave a little moan. It was too late now. They could never get up again; they would have to land. The rocket sank lower, skimming the tops of the sandhills. Then the inevitable end began.

She touched and sprang, twirling and twisting, end over end a hundred feet into the air, as though the planet had tried to hurl her back into the sky. She dropped. Again she was flung up like a huge spinning shuttle gleaming with flame and reflected sunlight. She fell for the third time into a belt of bushes, firing them as she bounced, bumped and slithered towards the canal beyond.

The embankment almost saved her. For an uncertain moment she teetered on the edge. Then she tilted and half rolled, half slid into the water. A huge frothy column rose into the purple sky and two hundred yards of the bank went out of existence as she blew up.

Vaygan watched the water pouring out over the desert and the flame racing along the line of dry bushes. But Joan saw nothing of this, for she had fainted.

CHAPTER XXI

HANNO

JOAN recovered to find Vaygan's arm supporting her while with his other hand he held a bowl for her to drink from. At the same time he was talking loudly, issuing instructions for the repair of the broken embankment and warning of the fire spreading through the bushes, apparently to the empty room.

As her eyes opened his tone changed and he looked at her anxiously.

'You're all right now?'

'I think so. It was silly of me to faint. I'm sorry.'

'Does it often happen?'

She shook her head. 'No. It was seeing that terrible crash.'

He looked at her as though he were puzzled.

'Emotion? Can emotion do that to you?' he said wonderingly.

'Do you mean to say that you've never seen anyone faint before?'

'Never. We don't.'

Joan looked over his shoulder at the wall beyond. The vision panel had resumed its customary smoky-grey appearance.

'That's a very wonderful instrument,' she said. 'But I don't like it. It spies on people.'

He seemed surprised that it was new to her, and amused when she told him that television on Earth needed a transmitter.

'But how primitive! This is much easier. Two beams are directed at once. The point where they meet is focused on the screen. By narrowing the beams their intensity is increased in a smaller field bringing the subject up to life-size if necessary. It is quite simple.'

Joan shook her head. 'It sounds complicated to me. I'm afraid I'm not very good at understanding things like that.'

He looked at her, and smiled. 'You say that, but what you really mean is: "I don't want to understand things like that." Why?'

'It's true,' she admitted. 'But why, I can't tell you. It's an instinct, I suppose. Perhaps I feel that if I understood too much of things I should become part of a thing myself, instead of a person. I'm afraid of losing something, but I don't know quite what—Or do you think that's merely the rationalization of a lazy mind?'

'No. You're mind is not lazy. But I don't understand you. What can you lose by knowing more? Surely, the more you know of things the more you master them?'

'Yes. I know that's sensible, but my instinct is against it. Perhaps I inherit it from primitive ancestors. They thought it dangerous to know too much, so they just worshipped or accepted. Perhaps we shall outgrow it. In fact, when it concerns something I really want to know about, like your running machines, I don't feel any of that reluctance to learn.'

'You shall see more of them soon. But first, won't you tell me what they were saying in your rocket? What was it all about, and why did they have those pieces of coloured cloth?'

'Coloured cloth? Oh, flags. Those are national emblems; they were put up to claim the territory.'

'You still have nations! How strange. We had nations long ago. Our children sometimes play at nations even now: it is a phase they go through. But tell me what they were saying.'

He listened with amusement as she took him in as much detail as she could remember through the exchanges between her companions and the Russians, but when she had finished, there was something wistful in his expression. For a time he did not speak, but sat with his eyes on the window, gazing unseeingly over the desert.

'What are you going to do? Do you think your people will ally with them?' she asked.

'That? Oh, I wasn't thinking of that. It was of men in your rocket and in the other: such men as we used to have here. The other is for the machines to decide, it is their world now.'

'"Their world,"' Joan repeated. 'Then the machines do rule you.'

'In a sense the machine must rule from the moment it is put to work. One surrenders to its higher efficiency—that is why it was made. But it is really truer to say that we co-exist.'

Joan got up. 'Won't you show me your machines? Let me see them at work—whatever it is that they do—then, perhaps, I shall understand better. I'm still not at home with the idea of an individual, independent machine.'

'It may help you to understand both of us and the machines,' Vaygan agreed.

They left the building together by way of the airlock which she had used the previous night. On Vaygan's insistence she was wearing a Martian space suit, a smaller edition of the one he wore himself. It was far less cumbersome than the overall from the ship, but the thin, silvery material of which it was made insulated her from the outer temperature completely, and the glass-like globe covering her head was far less tedious to wear than an oxygen mask. Thin diaphragms set in the globe could transmit her own voice and pick up external noises, and as she crossed the threshold of the outer doors she became aware of sounds of movement all about her.

No individual or particular noise predominated. The effect was rather a compound murmur, faint hummings, continuous clickings and scutterings mingling with the subdued harshness of dehumanized voices. It was not the steady rhythm of a machine shop with its mechanical purr and rattle, nor the hubbub of a crowded street on Earth, yet it seemed to hold something of the two.

Joan watched the six-legged machines scurrying across the open space in front of her. Some were carrying burdens in the tentacles, others held the tentacles coiled to their sides. Most of them moved at a similar constant speed, though now and then one obviously in a hurry would scamper past, skilfully weaving its way through the lines at twice the average pace. The sight of the interweaving streams of traffic and the kaleidoscopic shifting of bright moving parts had a dazzling, dizzying effect on her. She waited for the confusion which a collision must bring, but there were no entanglements. No two machines even touched, for though there was no mass control the precise judgment of each appeared to be infallible. For the first time she felt an inkling of what Vaygan had tried to tell her.

These were not machines as she knew them. They were not the advanced counterparts of anything on Earth, but something altogether new. They did not live, in her sense of the word, yet they were not inert metal. They were a queer hybrid between the sentient and the insentient.

And she could not quell a rising sense of misgiving and outrage; she was unable to silence the voice of prejudice and self-defence which, to crush the suspicion that these monsters might be better fitted to survive than were her own kind, insisted that they should not exist and that they were in some ill-defined, superstitious sense wrong.

An idea more fantastic, yet more acceptable to her prejudices, occurred to her.

'They haven't brains inside those cases?' she asked Vaygan beside her.

'Yes—— Oh, I see what you mean. No, we've never been able to transplant a human brain into a machine, though it has been tried. It would not have been very useful if it had succeeded. For instance, you would have seen a dozen collisions by now if human brains had been in charge. Our responses are not quick enough. You are wasting time by thinking anthropomorphically. The machines are—the machines.'

He led her across the open space (once, he told her, a garden which their utmost efforts had failed to preserve; now a waste, as aridly depressing as a parade ground) and turned into one of the wider streets which ran from it. Joan kept closely beside him, overcoming with difficulty the fear that the rushing mechanisms about them would trample them to death by a misjudgment. To the end she could never fully believe that their control was superior to her own, but she grew easier as she noticed how the traffic divided for them and that danger was never really imminent. After a short time she had recovered enough equanimity to listen to Vaygan's talk.

In its time, he was telling her, Hanno had been the home of between five and six million people. Nowadays the machines had adapted much of it for their own use while the rest stood empty save for the airtight building where the surviving men and women dwelt.

'Where are they?' Joan put in. 'I haven't seen anyone but you yet. When can I see the rest?'

'Perhaps tomorrow. They insist that you shall be medically examined first. You may easily be a carrier of Earth germs which would be fatal to us.'

'But if to them, why not to you?'

'Someone had to take the risk.' He smiled at her. 'I'm glad it was I.'

Joan hesitated. Then it became possible only to change the subject.

'Why are there none of them in the streets?'

He explained that the majority never left the central building. 'We can if we want to,' he added, 'but we seldom want to. We are almost museum pieces. They scarcely need us any longer.'

She frowned. 'They' evidently meant the machines.

'I know it must sound silly, but I still can't help thinking along my old lines. I don't understand why they haven't conquered you and wiped you out. And yet you, yourself, seem to think of them as friends—almost protectively.'

'Can you not bring yourself to see that machines are not the enemies, but the complements of mankind?—It is of your kind of machine I am talking now—Clearly you do not in the least appreciate what you have found. Humanity is flexible, machinery is not. If you do not adapt to it, it will conquer you. You must learn to use the controls of the car that is carrying you, or it will run away with you.' He paused, and then went on: 'But that applies to you to whom the machine is new. With us it is utterly different. You say our attitude to them is protective. That is true. They are our future—all the future we have. Did I not tell you that they are the children of our brains? They are the final extension of ourselves, so that we have every reason to be proud, not jealous of them.

'But circumstances on your Earth give another aspect. The larger planet has the longer life. Your race's day is far from done, so you are both jealous and afraid of the machines. It may be that you will be jealous of them to the end, for the end of man on Earth will not be like his end on Mars. Because our planet is small, the end has come early in evolution—no more natural forms can develop here. But Earth is barely in her middle age; there is time yet for many kinds of creatures to rule her. It may easily be that you will strangle yourselves with your own machines and thus make your own prophecies come true, and that another creature will arise to look back on man as man looks back on the reptiles.'

'No,' Joan's objection was a reflex. 'Mankind must be the peak.'

'What vanity! I tell you, the great Lords of the Earth are yet to come. They may evolve from man, or they may not. But if they do, they will not be men as we know them. There is change—always change. Even on this dying planet we are the instruments which have evolved new lords to come after us: perhaps they will make others to follow them. Do you really think that for all the millions of years to come you can face Nature unchanged? We have tried, and changed even as we tried. And now that we have made the machines to fight Nature we find that we are no more than the tools of that evolution which is Nature herself. We say we fight her while we do her bidding—the joke is on us.'

Vaygan led on. He showed her magnificent halls, bare and deserted, great libraries where were books printed upon imperishable sheets, but with the characters all but faded from the pages. She saw that long stretches of the shelves gaped empty. The machines had taken all of any use to them: the rest dealt with human beings—they were no longer needed. He took her through galleries which he himself had never seen before, filled with sculptures upon which the settling dust had mounted age by age. They went into theatres whose strange circular stages had known no actors for thousands of years. He tried, in a place not unlike a television or cinema theatre, to give her a glimpse of the thriving Hanno of long ago, but the machinery was corroded and useless. He showed her a hall filled with queer little cars which had once raced along the streets outside. She was surprised at the preservation of it all. A city on Earth neglected for a fraction of the time that Hanno had been empty would have fallen into mounds of ruin. Vaygan ascribed it partly to the dryness of Mars and the lack of growing things, and partly to the hardness of the materials.

'But, even so,' he said, 'if you look at the corners of the buildings you will see that they are not as sharp as they were. The wind has fretted the sand against them, but I think, in the end, that they will outlast the wind.'

They came to districts where they were completely alone, with the streets as empty as the buildings to either side of them. The effect was melancholy. Joan began to long for activity and movement again, even if it were only the bustle of the machines. She fancied that Vaygan, too, seemed relieved when she suggested that they should turn back.

'Now I will show you that part of Hanno which is not dead,' he said.

He took her into one of the factories where machines made more machines. She looked about it, hoping to understand a little of what was going on and vainly trying to change a lifetime's habits of thought. She felt that once her mind would accept the idea of a living machine as an accomplished fact she would be able to sympathize with Vaygan's attitude. But still her reason balked at it. To advance the theory in the living-room of the *Gloria Mundi* had been one thing: to accept the reality of it was quite another. Was it, she wondered, a part of that inadaptability Vaygan had spoken about? She followed thoughtfully as he led on into another hall.

'This is one of the repair shops,' he told her.

She noticed the different sections allotted to the mending or replacement of damaged tentacles, legs, lenses or other parts.

'There seem to be a lot of breakages,' she said.

'There are, but it doesn't matter. Once we tried giving the machines a more complex nervous system for their own protection. It worked, but we gave it up. It caused unnecessary pain when there was an accident, and the parts are very easily renewed. There is only one thing which we cannot replace, and that is memory, because each individual's memory is built up of his own accumulation of observations. If that is smashed, a fresh memory blank must be put in and the machine has to begin all over again. It is as near to death as a machine can come for it has lost everything which built its personality.'

Joan was reminded of a question which she had several times intended to ask:

'Those queer machines in the bushes and on the desert—there's nothing like them here. What are they?'

'Mistakes, mostly. Mistakes or experiments which have either escaped or been turned out there to see how they survive.'

'But why haven't you destroyed them?'

'They don't worry us and they seldom come near the cities. Usually they roam about in bands. You see, they have no factories and if anything goes wrong, they must rebuild themselves from one another's parts. There is still such a thing as luck in the world, and it's not impossible that the "mistakes" may prove valuable in teaching the rest something.

'The machines are by no means perfect yet—probably they never will be—so there are constant attempts to improve them. At one time we thought we could build a machine which need not start with blank memory plates. It would save the time spent in building memories—education, if you like to call it that. A groundwork of artificial memory was built in to give them a start—usually with deplorable results. Now we think it impossible, but for many years experimenters went on trying and it was during that time that most of the "mistakes" were created. If one takes these machines'—he waved a hand around him—'if one takes these as normal, one might say that those in the desert are mad. Nowadays we try (or, rather, the machines try, for they build themselves) very little tampering with mind.'

'Mind,' Joan repeated. 'I wish I could grasp that. A mechanical brain in control I find difficult to understand: a mechanical mind, impossible.'

Vaygan looked puzzled. 'Mind is the control of brain by memory—why should that be hard to understand?'

Joan gave it up. How could she explain one-tenth of her difficulties to a man who regarded machines as a race of beings differing from himself only in the material of their construction?

After her medical examination—an affair of blood-testing machines, mechanical ultra short-wave cameras and automatic response registers—Vaygan took her back to the room on the third level of the central building. She shed her air-suit and helmet with relief.

'When shall we know when I can meet the others?' she asked. He thought it likely that the reports of the tests would be made the next morning.

'And what about my friends?' she went on. 'What is happening to them?'

She half hoped that he would switch on the television panel again, but the idea did not seem to occur to him. He said:

'The machines are looking after them.'

'What do you think they will do?'

'They're going to send them back very soon.'

'What!'

'Certainly. Your friends could not live peacefully with our machines. They do not understand them. Nor could your people mix with ours; there is too much difference. Your race is young and ambitious; ours has that peace which the approach of death is said to give to the aged. As a race, we are resigned . . .'

He stood beside the window. The sunlight was slanting now. The spaces between the buildings were thrown into deep shadow, beyond them the arid red sand still sparkled as though it quivered.

'As a race . . .' Joan said. 'But you? What are you thinking as a man, Vaygan?'

His smile was wistful as he turned to her.

'I was not so much thinking as feeling—feeling history.'

'History?'

'The growing pains of young civilizations. Mars was not always old, you know. In its adolescence there were ambitions, wars, victories, defeats and, above all, hopes. It was a beautiful world. There were trees, animals, flowers; there were seasons when the leaves came and seasons when they fell; there were men and women in their millions. We have histories . . .

'But then, very many thousands of years ago Mars began to grow old. The water became scarcer and scarcer; that united us. For the first time in our history all the nations worked together, and they built the great canals which kept our soil fertile for many generations. But it was only a temporary victory. There were always desert patches, and as time went on they spread like a malignant disease. They drove back the plants until it was only on the canal banks that anything could grow.

'Our air grew thinner. It leaked slowly away into space until life in the open became impossible for us. We have put off the end in one way and another; clinging until the last as life always clings. We don't know why. Everything must end in time. In some hundreds of millions of years the sun itself will flicker for the last time and every trace of life will vanish from the system—yet we have struggled to preserve ourselves against our reason for a few generations longer. And so, in spite of all we have done and everything we know, we have come to a dwindling end; a few listless survivors who must spend their lives in a prison of their own building.

'I was thinking of all that we have lost: all that you still have. And of the things that I have never had. We are born old. I never knew the joy, energy and ambitions which are in youth—yet I know the loss and I feel that I have been robbed of my heritage. You can dream of the future and of your children's future: we can dream of nothing but the past. I think that I should be content with that as very old people are content, but I am not. I have seen the men of your race and I am jealous of them. Against my reason I resent the fate which has placed me in a dying world where existence has no features. It is as though a forgotten thing had revived in me. An unfamiliar stirring, or perhaps an empty aching impossible of fulfilment. I feel that I could cry out: "Give me life. Let me live before I die."'

He paused and looked at her again, searching her face.

'You don't understand—you can't understand. Youth flows in you; it rises in your veins as sap used to rise in our trees. It colours every thought of yours, this hope, this sense of the future. Even when you are old you will not feel the tired dry barrenness which we can never forget.'

'And yet,' Joan said gently, 'you are not speaking now as if life held nothing for you. You talked before as if you had forgotten emotion, and yet now——'

'I had. I had forgotten it. We must forget it in this world ... This is not the real Vaygan talking to you now; not the Vaygan you met last night. This is a younger Vaygan; the Vaygan who might have been—a million years ago. The Vaygan who dare not exist now lest he should die of discouragement.

'It is you who have done this to me. You and those others with you. But mostly you, yourself. You have given me a glimpse, a vision of people who still live. There is something—how shall I say?—a spirit in you and around you. It is the life force of young things striving, reaching out, still climbing upward to the peaks of life. We crossed those peaks long ago and we have been descending on the other side these thousands of years. Yet there is this thing which calls from you to me and stirs in me those vestiges of a Vaygan who in the long forgotten ages was joyously scaling those peaks with no knowledge of the futility which lay beyond. This thing almost makes me think against my better knowledge that the end is not just the coldness of universal cinders. I feel now that only to have lived would have been an achievement—perhaps only to have died, like those men in the rocket. At least they knew hope before they died.'

Joan said nothing. She barely followed his words and their meaning was lost, but with her eyes on his she saw more than he told. His hands took hers, trembling a little. His broad chest rose and fell with deeper breaths. It seemed to her as though a lay figure of a man were coming to life.

'You!' he whispered. 'You have lent me life for a little while. You have fanned a spark which was almost dead, and it hurts me, Joan. It hurts me . . .'

CHAPTER XXII

A SIEGE IS RAISED

DUGAN knocked up a switch and the spare bulb of the searchlight mounted at the window in a temporary reflector went dead. He snatched up a pair of field-glasses and pointed them at the group on the sandhill close by the bushes. For some minutes he watched the flashes from a bright piece of metal held in a man's hand. Then he lowered the glasses, flashed out the sign for 'message received' on the searchlight bulb, and turned to the others.

'They say their air supply is good for another eight hours yet,' he said.

The four looked at one another.

'Well, *is* there anything we can do?' asked the doctor.

'Damned if I can think of it,' Dale muttered.

Froud looked again at the party on the sandhill. In

the dry air it was possible to make out even at that distance the overalled figures of the four Russians and the ring of imprisoning machines.

'I'm feeling a bit of a swine,' he said. 'Sheer human decency ought to have made us warn them. Instead, I just encouraged Karaminoff to go head first into trouble.'

'I shouldn't worry about that. They wouldn't have believed us, and they were bound to meet the machines sooner or later,' the doctor told him.

Froud grunted. 'Maybe. All the same there's a hell of a difference between trying to save a man and shoving him in. However, he did at least have the sense to get back when he saw what was coming out of the bushes. But what the devil can we do about it? They've got them the same way as they got us. They've been there nearly six hours now, and it's not likely they'll be interrupted this time...' He broke off. 'Hi, Dugan, they're flashing.'

Dugan put up his glasses once more. After a minute:

'Can't read it. Must be signalling their own ship again,' he announced.

Froud pressed his face against the window in an effort to look astern. The fact that the window was set in the curving bow restricted his field, but he could see enough —half a dozen of the grotesquely assembled machines posted unmovingly opposite the entrance port.

'Still there,' he said gloomily. He crossed the room and sat down on the side of one of the couches. 'This is a hell of a mess. It's dead certain that if we go out there we'll get caught too, and that won't help anybody. But if we're ever going to get away, we've got to get out sooner or later to upend the ship—and that's going to be no light job. Seems to me as if Joan and Burns had the better deal, after all—at least it was over quickly ... Why the devil can't they let us alone, anyway?'

'To divide their planet between us?' asked the doctor.

'Rot. Those things out there can't reason like that. If they were human beings, there'd be some sense in their resentment. But machines ... I ask you, why should machines attack us at sight?'

'Metal, I think,' Dugan contributed unexpectedly. 'They seem to be short of it. You saw how they rebuilt themselves from one another's parts. They could get a lot of metal from a ship like this.'

'That's true,' Froud agreed. 'With us out of the way they could break her up. I wonder if you've hit it?'

'I suppose it wouldn't be possible for us to remove ourselves?' the doctor suggested tentatively. 'I mean, to shoot the G.M. along the ground by use of the tail rockets?'

'We'd be more likely to dig into a sandhill and bury ourselves on a surface like this,' Dale thought.

'And it wouldn't do us much good if we did move a few miles,' Froud added. 'Our friends the nickel-plated nightmares would just come along too.'

'Well, damn it all, we can't just sit here doing nothing,' Dugan said explosively. But he offered no alternative. Nor, it seemed, could anyone else. For a time an uninspired silence hung over the room.

'It's all so darned silly,' Froud murmured at last, 'that's what gets me down. We push off with world acclaim, we successfully avoid all the perils of space and arrive here safely only to find (a) that the place is over-run with idiotic-looking machines; (b) that two other rockets have also pushed off, but without the acclaim; and (c) that our only safety from the said idiotic machines is to stay bottled up in here. It simply isn't good enough. It's not at all the sort of thing that put Raleigh and Cook in the history books.'

'Besides,' said the doctor, 'think of the yarns of hero-ism you'll have to invent for public consumption if ever we do get back.'

Dugan began to flash his light again.

'Asking if their ship's still bottled up too,' he explained.

They watched him transmit, and receive his answer.

'Well?' asked Dale.

'Yes. They left two men aboard the *Tovaritch* and machines are now parking round the entrance to keep 'em there. The two they sent back—the one I pipped and the other—don't seem to have turned up. Either the machines have jumped on them, or they're holding out somewhere behind those dunes.'

'Then there were eight altogether on the *Tovaritch*. Pretty good,' Dale admitted grudgingly.

'It's a pity,' remarked Froud, 'that nobody thought to load a few hand grenades. One or two among that bunch by the door ought to tangle 'em up enough to put 'em out of action——' He paused as if a new thought had struck him. 'I say,' he went on excitedly, 'why don't we make some? There are enough explosives on board of one kind and another, God knows.'

They all turned to Dale. He thought for a moment.

'All right. I expect some more machines will turn up, but it's worth trying.'

'Anyway, it may give us long enough to get Kara-minoff and Co. out of their jam,' Dugan agreed. 'I'll signal him what we're doing, and he can pass it on to the men on the *Tovaritch* to do the same.'

'Pity we can't signal them direct,' Dale said. He looked out of the other window. 'If she'd only landed a few feet farther to the left we could have seen her windows and there wouldn't be any need for this three-cornered——' He broke off suddenly as a string of machines came scuttling at top speed round the flank of an intervening sandhill. 'Hullo, what the devil's happening now?'

The others crowded up to him. They watched the machines swerve on to a course headed for the bushes. A moment later they were followed by a dozen or so more, also travelling fast. Away to the left Froud noticed a series of reflected flashes crossing the crest of another dune.

'More active ironware on the way,' he announced. 'What the dickens is up now? Whatever it is, these nearer chaps don't seem to care for it. Watch their dust.'

The unwieldy cavalcade lumbered past, making the best speed its ill-assorted parts would allow. Froud dashed across to the other window.

'The ones round Karaminoff are sheering off, too,' he reported. 'Streaking for the——'

'Good God!' said Dugan's voice. 'Look at that!'

He pointed wildly at an object which had suddenly made an appearance on the top of the dune between themselves and the other ship. A strange, tank-like device supported by innumerable short legs which ended in wide round plates. It stopped abruptly on the crest. The sunlight reflecting from its curved casework and the glittering of its lenses made it hard to look at. A sudden discharge of bright blue flashes snapped from its bows, and immediately consternation smote the fleeing machines. There were no missiles, no visible causes for the turmoil into which they were thrown, yet the disorganization was complete. They lost their course and began to run this way and that with a wild, senseless flourishing of tentacles and jointed levers. Their ill-matched legs bore them on erratic lines so that they fouled one another and crashed ponderously together. A number tripped and fell, breaking or twisting the legs of others. There was a fresh salvo of flashes from the large machine, and the confusion grew. Had such a thing been possible, the crew of the *Gloria Mundi* would have said that they were watching machines go mad. They became a berserk mass of milling, flailing metal, surging this way and that, hopelessly tangled and interlocked, crashing and buffeting back and forth in an insane mellay. The tank-like contrivance trundled down the hill, still emitting its blue flashes and driving the machines to even greater frenzies of self-destruction. A dozen or more coffin-shaped objects ran in its wake. Except for the lack of one pair of legs they were identical with that in Joan's pictures.

'Well, thank Heaven for some machines which look as if they had been built by men who were at least fairly sane,' said Dugan.

'Allegory,' said Froud. 'Order putting paid to Chaos.'

'But why should there be chaotic machines at all?' asked the doctor.

'Why,' Froud countered, 'should Chaos ever have existed?'

The big machine ceased its fusillade. The recent besiegers appeared to have reduced themselves to a few heaps of scrap metal. Froud admired the efficiency of the operation. He said admiringly:

'You know, that's one of the bigger ideas. Just send your opponents potty, and watch them wipe one another out. We must take the notion back with us. Now, what do you suppose happens next?'

CHAPTER XXIII

EXPULSION

At first Joan did not know why she awoke. The room was silent and dark. Vaygan had not woken. She lay still and quiet, pressed against his side, with her head on his shoulder, listening to his breathing; her left arm lay across his chest, rising and falling gently with its rhythm. Then, gradually she became aware of another sound—a faint, familiar humming somewhere close by which told her that a machine was in the room. She held her breath to listen, and then relaxed. What did it matter? Let the machines run about like the silly toys they were. They no longer had any importance.

There was a cold touch on her shoulder, and a harsh, metallic voice spoke out of the darkness. She sat up swiftly. Vaygan woke too as his arm fell from about her. He put his hand over hers.

'What is it?' he asked.

'A machine,' she said, almost in a whisper. 'It touched me.'

With his other hand he found the switch, and the ceiling diffused a gradually increasing light. The machine was standing close beside the bed with its cold, blank lenses turned full on them.

'What is it?' Vaygan repeated, but this time he asked the question of the machine.

As before, Joan was unable to follow the harsh rapidity of its mechanical speech, but she watched the expressions on Vaygan's face as he listened, and her heart sank. After a few questions which involved lengthy answers he turned to her. She knew from the look in his eyes what he was going to say before she heard the words.

'The medical report was unfavourable—you carry dangerous bacteria. It says that you will have to go.'

'No, Vaygan. It's wrong. I'm healthy and clean.'

He took both her hands in his.

'My dear, it is true. The tests can't lie. I was afraid of it. The Earthly bacteria you carry might start a disease here which would wipe all my people out—and you, they say, are not immune from many of the bacteria we carry. It would be both suicide and murder for your people and mine to mix.'

'But you and I, Vaygan. We——?'

He agreed softly. 'I know, my dear—I know.'

'Oh, let me stay. Let me stay here with you . . .'

'It is not possible. They say you must go.'

'They?—The Machines?'

'Not just the Machines. My people say it.'

Joan dropped back and hid her face in the pillow. Vaygan slid one arm round her bare shoulders. With his other hand he stroked her hair.

'Joan. Joan. Listen. You could not stay here. Even mixing with us you could not live our life—for you it would be only a slow death. You would be lonely as no one has ever been lonely before. Your heart would break, my dear—and mine, too, I think. I could not stand seeing you crushed by hopelessness. The very old and the very young have nothing to share. For a few moments you and I have met. For a time at least I have known through you how I might have lived; almost I have known how it feels to belong to a race in its youth. Now it is finished, but I shall never forget, for you have given me something which is beautiful beyond all I ever dreamed.'

Joan raised her face and looked at him through tears. 'No, Vaygan. No. They can't make me go now. A few days—a week. Can't they let us have just a week?'

The voice of the machine broke in harshly.

'It says that there is not much time,' Vaygan told her. 'The rocket must start just after dawn, or it will have to wait another day.'

'Make it wait, Vaygan. Keep me here and make it wait one more day.'

'I couldn't if I would.' He looked at the machine. 'It's their world now, and they don't want you. That is the message you are to take back to Earth with you. Earth is to leave Mars alone. Some years ago they sent a ship to Earth to prospect, and when it came back, that was their decision. They mean it, Joan.'

But she seemed not to hear him. She put up her hand and gripped his shoulder.

'Vaygan, you shall come back with us. Why shouldn't you come back? There'll be room in the *Gloria Mundi*. I can persuade Dale to take you—you can get him some more fuel if necessary. Yes, you must. Oh, say you'll come, Vaygan, my dear.'

He looked sadly into her face.

'I can't, Joan.'

'But you must. Oh, you shall.'

'But, my darling, don't you see? I must not mix with your race any more than you with mine.'

He slipped from the bed. He stood beside it for a moment, looking down at her. Then he pulled the coverlet aside and picked her up. She clung to him.

'Oh, Vaygan. Vaygan.'

'Hoy!' said Dugan. 'You're the prize scholar. What's this chap trying to tell us?'

Froud joined him at the window and together they watched the antics of the machine below. It was scratching characters very busily on a carefully smoothed piece of ground.

'Quite a little sand artist, isn't he?' Froud said. 'As far as I can see, it's an instruction that we must leave one something after dawn.'

'What do you mean—"one something"?'

'I suppose it's a measure of time of some kind.'

'Very helpful. Hi, Dale!'

'What is it?' Dale looked up irritably from his calculations.

'Sailing orders, but we can't read 'em.'

'Well, if you can't, you can't. My reckoning came out at one hour and twenty minutes after dawn, which means that we've now got'—he glanced at the clock—'thirty-two minutes to go.'

Froud drifted over to another window. Across the intervening dunes he could see the *Tovaritch* glistening in the early light. Like the *Gloria Mundi* she had been raised to the perpendicular with her blunt nose pointing to the sky. He frowned, wondering how the machines had accomplished the erection in so short a time, wondering too if the occupants of the *Tovaritch* had also suffered the indignity of being flung in a heap as the ship suddenly tilted beneath them.

'There's one thing I can't forgive,' he muttered to no one in particular,' 'and that's their keeping us bottled in here while they tipped it up. I'd have given a lot to see how they did it, and to get some pictures of it.'

'It was too dark for pictures, anyhow,' the doctor told him consolingly, 'but I do wish they'd given us some warning. Nearly cracked my skull on the floor as we went up. Would have done if one wasn't so light here.'

Froud took no notice of him. He was going on:

'I've covered a few dud assignments in my time, but of all the flops, this is the floppiest. We come here, we get chased about by crazy machines and we get told to go home again by slightly less crazy machines. We don't know what makes them work, who made them, how they made them, where they made them, when they made them, nor why they made them. In fact, we don't know a blasted thing, and the whole outing has been too damn' silly for words. We've lost Joan, poor kid, and Burns was laid out for nothing. If this is interplanetary exploration, give me archaeology.'

'On the other hand,' the doctor put in, 'we know that life still exists here by the canals. I've got some specimens, you've got some photographs. Dale has proved that it is possible to make a flight between——'

'Hullo!' Froud interrupted. 'Here's something in a hurry, just look at it.' He watched a bright speck tearing towards them and covering the successive lines of dunes at a prodigious pace.

'It looks different from the rest. I believe it's carrying something. Where are those glasses? It is. It's holding a man in those tentacle things. It's coming here. Stand by the airlock, Dugan.'

Dugan obediently pulled over the lever for the outer door.

'How's he going to reach it——?' he began, but a shout from Froud cut him short.

'It isn't. It's Joan. Joan!' He dropped the glasses and waved frantically. An arm lifted in reply as the machine passed round the rocket and out of his sight.

All four of them crowded round the inner door of the airlock watching for the glow of the indicator.

'How are they going to get her up to it?' Dugan asked anxiously.

'Don't you worry. A little thing like that's not going to—— There!' Froud finished as the warning light switched on. Dugan pulled over his lever and turned the valve-wheel. A few seconds later the door opened and Joan stepped out.

She did not seem to notice their welcome. She unscrewed her glass-like helmet and slipped off her overall suit without heeding the questions fired at her. When she looked up they saw that she was crying.

'Please, not now. I'll tell you later,' she said.

They watched in astonished silence as she ran to the trap-door and disappeared into the room below. At last Froud scratched his head ruefully. He bent down and picked up the silvery suit she had dropped.

'Now where on earth—on Mars, I mean—do you suppose that she got hold of this?'

Joan lay on the couch in the little cabin. She was speaking softly in a voice which did not reach to the other room. He had promised that he would switch on the screen. She knew that in that room, far away in Hanno, her face was looking at him from the wall and her voice whispering in his ears. She had so much to tell him—so many might-have-beens . . .

It seemed no more than a minute or two before Dale's voice called:

'Couches everyone!' and, 'Don't forget your straps, Joan.'

'All right,' she told him weakly as her hands reached for them.

Only a few minutes left. She whispered more urgently in the empty room. Seconds now. She could hear Dale counting the past away, slowly and deliberately . . .

'Five—four—three—two—one——'

'Oh, Vaygan. Vaygan . . .'

CHAPTER XXIV

FINALE

THE story of the *Gloria Mundi*'s return is well known. Since even the schoolbooks will tell you how she landed in North Africa on the seventh of April, 1982, with only a litre or two of spare fuel in her tanks, it is unnecessary for me to give a detailed account. And if you want figures to explain why the return journey took seventy days whereas the outward journey took seventy-four, or if you want to know how many minutes and seconds more than forty hours she spent on Mars, I cannot do better than refer you again to *The Bridging of Space* which Dale has crammed with vast (and, to me, indigestible) quantities of mathematical and technical information.

The experiences of her crew and particularly those of Joan started arguments which are not dead yet, for while one school of thought regards them as evidence that man on Mars has really mastered the machine and used it for his own ends, the other adduces them as proving the direct opposite. And there, for lack of corroborative detail, the matter see-saws to the contempt of a third body of opinion which does not believe a word of their stories and declares that the whole flight was a hoax.

In the early excitement of their return it was enough for the people of Earth that man had at last flung his first flimsy feeler into space. Dale and his crew were fêted; even the learned societies rivalled one another in honouring them, and never perhaps has so great a publicity value been attached to so few names.

And never before, thought Mary Curtance, had the floodlight on the Curtance family reached one-tenth of its present candle-power. But now, in the months of waiting, she had learnt to tolerate it with a better grace; she accepted it for Dale's sake and kept secret her hope that the noise and the shouting would soon die away. It was a hope destined to be granted far sooner than she expected.

The carping spirit, which accused the expedition in general and Joan in particular of failing to take full advantage of the chances, began to show itself very soon, and the swing of popular opinion from hero-worship to recrimination was as painful as it was surprising. The animosity against Joan was said to have its origin in the American refusal to believe her report of the wreck of their rocket. Be that as it may, within a few weeks she was incurring revilement and persecution for every one of her actions since the start. In a few short days she fell from the position of a heroine to, at best, a liar and a waster of opportunities. It was no good that the others should stand by her. They were shouted down. Nor was it considered sufficient excuse that Froud should say:

'What right have you to blame the girl? She's human. Why, damn it, when the last trump blows half the women will miss it because they are in the middle of some love-affair.'

The gale of public opinion was dead against her and she could only run for shelter.

Out of Russia, too, came trouble in the form of a rumour that Dale had deliberately disabled the *Tovaritch* on Mars and left Karaminoff and his crew there to die. And as the weeks and months passed away without sign of her the slander gained wider credence.

And so ended the flight of the *Gloria Mundi*.

It was five years before the public mind could forget its pettiness and reinstate Dale in a position analogous with that of Christopher Columbus. Dugan, Froud and Doctor Grayson shared with him in this return to public esteem, but Joan did not.

Six months after the *Gloria Mundi*'s return, in a little cottage among the Welsh mountains, Joan had died in giving birth to her child. But the tale of Vaygan's son belongs to a different story.

THE SECRET PEOPLE

JOHN WYNDHAM
writing as JOHN BEYNON

The planners of the world's greatest engineering feat—the flooding of part of the Sahara desert—knew nothing of the life which teemed below their New Sea. But for the accident which plunged Mark Sunnet and his girl-friend into a cavernous world, nothing would have been known of the catastrophe which now threatened the survivors of an ancient race. Their struggle against doom, and Mark's fight for survival, is the theme of this fascinating story.

HIS FIRST FULL-LENGTH NOVEL—NOW
PUBLISHED IN PAPERBACK FOR
THE FIRST TIME

THE UNCERTAIN MIDNIGHT

EDMUND COOPER

**They called him the Survivor—
a 20th Century man 'reborn' in 2113**

After a devastating atomic holocaust, mankind had now turned to the machine to solve his problems. Which led to the androids—descended from the robot, they were hardly distinguishable from real humans. By the year 2113 they ran society—leaving man to a life of leisure.

It was into this world that John Markham emerged after spending 146 years of suspended animation in an underground deep-freeze unit. But his new lease on life was likely to be a short one. A man with his 'outdated' ideas could be very dangerous—a fact the androids realized only too well . . .

'He writes with great authority and skill'

Arthur C. Clarke

FROM THE ACKNOWLEDGED MASTERS
OF SCIENCE FICTION

John Wyndham

☐ 15834 4   THE SECRET PEOPLE   30p

Edmund Cooper

☐ 02860 2   ALL FOOL'S DAY   17½p

☐ 15091 2   THE LAST CONTINENT   25p

☐ 15132 3   THE UNCERTAIN MIDNIGHT   25p

☐ 10904 1   FIVE TO TWELVE   25p

☐ 12975 1   SEA-HORSE IN THE SKY   25p

John Christopher

☐ 02716 9   A WRINKLE IN THE SKIN   17½p

☐ 10858 4   PENDULUM   25p

Kurt Vonnegut

☐ 02876 9   THE SIRENS OF TITAN   17½p

CORONET BOOKS, HODDER PAPERBACKS, Cash Sales Department, Kernick Industrial Estate, Penryn, Cornwall.

Please send cheque or postal order, no currency, and allow 5p per book (4p per copy on orders of five copies and over) to cover the cost of postage and packing in U.K., 5p per copy overseas.

Name ....

Address ....

....